I0690590

Tales of the Macrofurs
Volume 1: The Big Boys

First Edition

Published by The Nazca Plains Corporation
Las Vegas, Nevada
2010

ISBN: 978-1-935509-79-0
Ebook: 978-1-61098-010-4

Published by

The Nazca Plains Corporation ®
4640 Paradise Rd, Suite 141
Las Vegas NV 89109-8000

PUBLISHER'S NOTE
Tales of the Macrofurs is a work of fiction created wholly by *Rogue*'s
imagination. All characters are fictional and any resemblance to any
persons living or deceased is purely by accident. No portion of this
book reflects any real person or events.

Cover Artwork by
Crux Lo

Art Director, Blake Stephens

Tales of the Macrofurs
Volume 1: The Big Boys

First Edition

Rogue

Contents

Foreword

It is a primordial fact that size is everything. Humankind has always had an inherent fascination with giants. Ancient myths are filled with them. Legendary characters are ten feet tall. We feel a visceral sort of thrill when gazing up at something we see as powerful, overwhelming, enormous, as though some racial memory has survived the eons since we were tiny balls of fluff scampering at the feet of dinosaurs. Godzilla movies have been wildly popular for decades, but can it really be for the fascinating plots and gripping dialogue? Heck, no. Godzilla stomps gleefully across that part of our brain that yearns for someone to look up to – *way* up to.

Sometimes, too, those giants find their way into darker parts of our mind where many fear to venture. A giant, particularly a very big one, can do what he wants and usually does so despite the efforts of sissy fairy-tale heroes. He is an overwhelming force, the personification of dominance over others. Deep inside of us, whether or not we choose to acknowledge it, there is a desire to possess that power, that freedom, that ultimate control...or perhaps even to be subjugated to it. For some, that desire is sufficiently powerful to warrant its own name, and having found none to my liking in 1986, I coined one on my own: *macrophile*, the lover of great size. I never dreamed that I would one day find it in a dictionary.

Sadly for us, there have never been true giants among the human ranks save for the occasional circus attraction. Nature, though, provides them in abundance. Saurian voices once bellowed from on high. Mammoths wandered the plains until recent geological memory, and today their descendants plod across the Savannah and mourn their inevitable passing at the hands of Man. That is the sad fate of all of Nature's giants. In spite of their size and their strength, they will inevitably lose out to those with the brains and the opposable thumbs. What, though, if that portion of the playing field were to be stomped flat? What if those towering creatures from the Wild could think on our level? What if they could walk upright and plan and communicate and grasp small objects – like people – with fine motor control? What chance would the descendants of the tree-shrew stand then?

That is where Rogue comes in. Ninety feet of humanoid wolf came raging across the virtual worlds of the Internet some twenty years ago and very quickly became something of a cult icon among those who had begun to identify themselves as *macrophiles*. He was an unstoppable, overwhelming force of nature who could think and plan and pick up cars and laugh raucously as he stepped on people – and in short order he attracted a worldwide fan club numbering in the thousands. No matter how savage, no matter how vicious, no matter how depraved his attacks on Humanity, they just kept lining up for more. He had become a furry Godzilla, both feared and adored by his would-be victims.

Others followed in his colossal footsteps, leading to the coining of yet another word: *macrofur.* As time went on many of their stories were set down in prose to which Rogue put his name. His corner of the Internet was filled not only with the smoking ruins of once-great cities but with a vast library of tales in which Nature's fury is unleashed on those who have lost their tenuous advantage. Many of the giant beasts of his creation flaunt their sovereignty over those they see as paltry and weak just as their natural counterparts would: by sexual domination, a practice shared by most species of an evolutionary level higher than the amoeba. Conquering, controlling, even destroying another with the force of virility alone is deeply ingrained in any species that has had to fight for its survival. That includes most of them with the exception of Mankind, who with his clever brain and nimble thumbs has not had to do that much fighting of late. We remember, however, even as our civilized minds try to deny it. Who knows what the dinosaurs might have done to our tiny ancestors given the capacity to feel contempt?

Read on. You will find out. Be forewarned, however, that in the world of the macrofurs human beings are little more than insects, and insects all too frequently wind up getting squashed, or worse. The tales that follow have been arranged in such a fashion that the reader is introduced first to giants with a more gentle disposition and then to those with increasingly malevolent intent. Read only as far as you dare, and never forget that the deeper you venture into those shadowy corners of the psyche, the greater the danger that you will fall prey to the colossal beasts that dwell there and never return.

Fire, Ice, and Sin

Kong was the only word Brian could think of to describe the man at the gate. Each of his arms was bigger around than Brian's waist. "This doesn't look like you," he growled, squinting.

Brian tried not to stammer. His driver's license looked like a postage stamp clutched in the man's meaty fingers. "Honest!" he said. "I let my hair grow out. Look, see?" He slid his mop back with both hands and pressed it tight to his head. "How's that?"

Kong squinted harder. "You sure you're eighteen?"

Andrew, who reeked of marijuana and was almost sure to get all of them thrown out, threw an arm around Brian's shoulder. "Come on, Man! Give him a break. It's his birthday today. Our little boy is finally a man! Tell you what: let's..."

"Yeah, yeah, whatever." Kong thrust the license back into Brian's hands. "Happy birthday, Kid." He waved the group impatiently through. "Next! Come on, keep it moving," he barked at the hundreds who had piled up behind.

Brian sighed with relief, even though he was still not sure he was all that happy to be there. It was nice of his housemates to take him out for his eighteenth, but this place definitely did not look like his type of scene. It did not help that none of them would give him even a clue what sort of place this was. "A club" was all that they would tell him. What kind of bullshit was that? They were in the middle of nowhere, surrounded by trees, no sign of a building anywhere around, and with enough chain link and barbed wire to make it look like he was being checked into a concentration camp.

Andrew must have sensed Brian's uneasiness. "Come on, Babyface, you're gonna love it!" He craned his neck and called back to the other two. "You dumbfucks didn't forget anything, did you?"

"Who are you calling a dumbfuck, Dumbfuck?" Brant nodded to the overstuffed bags he had been hauling around since the parking lot. "Plastic sheets, rainslickers times four, wet-naps, check. Kurt's got the markers and foamcore under his arm."

Brian was even more worried now. "This isn't that show where the guy smashes watermelons with a sledgehammer, is it?" he groaned.

Kurt and Brant burst out laughing while Andrew laid a brotherly hand on Brian's shoulder. "My son," he said somberly, "watermelons are for children." He grinned mischievously and tousled Brian's hair. "Today you are a man!"

The fence on either side of them narrowed to an alley that forced them to walk in single-file. A man with the faded words "event staff" stenciled on his shirt brandished a fistful of cheap pens in one hand and a stack of papers in another. "Releases!" he barked. "Take one and pass'em along, Folks. No admission without a signed release.

Releases! Take one and pass'em along, Folks. No admission without a signed release."

Brian peered at the minute legalese. "Indemnify and hold harmless... any and all...injuries...damage to person or property. Jeezus, Guys, what have you gotten me into?"

"Relax, Boy, just relax! It's just some legal bullshit that they need to have from everyone." Andrew thrust a pen into Brian's hand. "Just sign it and trust me. Nobody's ever gotten seriously hurt at one of these things."

"Not seriously, anyway," Kurt piped up.

"Ignore him, Brian," Andrew crooned. "Just sign the stupid thing. Come on, there's people waiting."

Reluctantly, Brian scrawled his signature. Within seconds he was being whisked through the gate and into a huge open field packed with humanity and brilliantly lit by blazing stadium lights all around. "Hey, where's the stage?" He stumbled a little as Andrew dragged him by the arm and the others pushed from behind. "And where's the seats?"

His friends only laughed. Behind him he heard Kurt snickering, "Oh, Man, he's going to totally freak out!" and then he was hemmed in by people on all sides. The crowd was cheering, shrieking, and surging from one side to the other while a raucous beat thudded from speakers somewhere on the far side of the fence.

"Here, put this on!" Andrew said, handing Brian a cheap plastic raincoat, one of those that comes in a package the size of a matchbook that it can never fit into again. "Keep the hood up. Believe me, you'll need it."

Kurt and Brant were already wearing theirs, and Kurt was even sporting a pair of safety goggles swiped from Professor Malkov's chemistry lab. All around them others were donning similar gear, while a few looked ready to brave the elements unprotected.

The blaring lights abruptly dimmed and the crowd let out a roar. "Ladies and Gentlemen!" a voice intoned. "They're huge, they're unbelievable, and they're here! Give it up for the wildest, the sexiest, the most gargantuan sex-kittens ever to walk to the face of the Earth: Fire, Ice, and Sin!"

The noise of the crowd was nearly drowned out by a raucous electric guitar riff that echoed four times while spots swirled crazily and the stadium lights flashed as though an epileptic had taken hold of the switch, and then abruptly everything went dark. A few female voices squealed and were answered by rude cackles. The speakers droned an ominous bass progression that was punctuated by a heavy thud that for some reason brought a new round of cheers and hoots from the crowd. Brian peered into the darkness but could not even make out the silhouette of anyone around him. He could hear Andrew giggling, though, and tried to stick close.

That thud came again and the music began to build, then another thud that Brian could feel through his legs. Another, stronger now, and another, stronger still. They came more frequently, each one heavier than the last, until it seemed the ground under Brian's feet was being shaken apart. The music reached a dramatic and grating crescendo. The stadium lights faded in and then blared blindingly.

The crowd went wild. All that Brian could say was "Jesus Fucking Christ!"

They stood with their backs to the crowd, their lean bodies clad only in short, dense fur whose striking colors made it clear how they had gotten their names. Fire and Ice stood on opposite sides of the field to the east and west, with midnight-black Sin standing due north. Brian had not seen any stage when he entered because no stage was needed. Each of the three stood taller than a ten story building.

Andrew suddenly seized Brian's arm. "What do you think, Man?" he laughed. "Is this fucking awesome or what?"

"What the hell are they?" Brian sputtered. "Are they...are they animatronic or something? They're moving!"

The music had switched to a low and pounding beat to which the giants began to sway in unison. As their hips rocked from side to side their long, furry tails swung with a low swooshing sound. A few eager spectators kept jumping up and trying to touch the tails as they swept overhead. The music swelled, as did the motion of the massive bodies, their shoulders rolling now.

Brian's eyes trailed along Ice's back, where the bright blue fur flowed like ocean waves over rippling muscles beneath, past the round curves of the giant's rump, and his breath caught. Something else was swaying in the darkness just beyond the reach of the stadium lights, between the giant's thighs. "Fucking Hell," he choked. "Is that...?"

"Just keep watching," Andrew giggled, and then turned to Kurt. "Twenty bucks says he pukes!"

Kurt's response went unheard beneath the ringing onslaught of thousands of voices hollering at the same time. All three giants turned at once to face into the crowd. Brian felt as though a hot poker was being run through his gut. They were feline, all of them, their ears tall and pointy, muzzles whiskered, eyes glittering with slit-pupiled mischief. The rest of them were human enough apart from the fur, right down to the part that kept Brian from noticing anything else. "Enormous" did not begin to tell the story. Between each one's legs swung a slab of meat as big as an SUV.

"Oh, man, he's gonna lose it!" Kurt guffawed. "You owe me twenty bucks, Dude!"

Brian held on, though, while the giants danced to the music, their svelte forms gyrating in place, their immense members swinging with audible slaps against their thighs, and the crowd howling its appreciation through it all until the final chord brought them out in thundering applause. Smiling coyly, the giants folded their arms over their chests and held themselves perfectly motionless until the next song fired up. As the opening chords blasted from the speakers Sin unfolded his arms and lowered them to his sides, fists clenched. Curling his muzzle into a smirk, he slowly lowered his gaze to the crowd, and even more slowly he raised a massive foot and swung it forward, its shadow falling upon the heads of those below.

"Holy shit!" Brian cried out, but he could not hear his own words over the crowd. He expected to see people clawing at one another in sudden panic as the great paw pads began to descend, but instead the crowd neatly parted to create a gap into which the giant's foot fit almost perfectly as it landed. Sin's muscles bulged as his weight shifted onto that foot and rolled forward with his next step. The tips of his toes swept low over the crowd, most of whom ducked down while others reached up and swatted at the passing digits in miniscule high-fives. His foot halted, poised aloft, while below it the crowd again pushed back and cleared just enough room for it to come down, its impact sending a murmuring shudder through the earth.

The crowd behind Brian suddenly pushed forward and he stumbled, fighting to keep his balance. He twisted around, ready to belt someone for roughhousing with him, when the reason for the surge became terrifyingly clear. So fixated had he been on Sin that he had not seen Fire wading into the crowd behind him. Now, all that he could see was the red feline's muscular leg rising like a pillar of flame nearby. Overhead the sole of Fire's foot hovered ominously, practically filling the sky. Somewhere he heard someone shouting, "Move it, move it!" and he allowed himself to be hustled out of the way.

An oblong patch of open grass formed, growing wider and wider as the spectators pushed back, the shadow of the descending foot falling into it. There was a low thud and the ground shook as Fire's heel impacted the ground. When his toes began to fall there was a flash of movement and a spectator stumbled awkwardly forward, falling on his face right in the shadow of the descending foot. Before anyone could react, the great toes came down and the spectator vanished from view. A collective gasp rose from the crowd. Someone screamed.

Fire did not even flinch. His towering leg shifted back and his toes lifted skyward again, his foot rocking back on its heel. The crowd shouted with relief when the spectator, dazed but apparently intact, crawled shakily from beneath the looming pads and emerged back into the light, where he was helped to his feet and dusted off by his cohorts.

"Whoa," someone next to Brian said shakily. "Did you see that?"

"Now you know why you signed a release," someone else answered.

With the way clear Fire stepped down again, this time letting his full weight ease forward onto his toes. His heel lifted and his foot rose smoothly into the air, leaving an impression behind into which people poured, erasing any sign that a giant had just passed through. Brian stared straight upward as the firm rump flexed, the giant's tail sweeping and dancing behind to help maintain the balance that had no doubt kept that hapless spectator alive. He was still staring as the great curves tensed and began to sink toward the ground. Brian thought for a moment that the titan was going to sit on the crowd, but instead Fire settled carefully down into a squat. The tip of his colossal penis dropped into the midst of the crowd and there was a frenzy of activity as little figures crowded around and began to press themselves against it, caressing, fawning, some even licking.

Kurt made an exaggerated retching sound. "Oh God, here's where it really starts to get sick!" he sneered. "Hey, Brian, you wanna go up there and help them?"

"Heh. No way," Brian said. He tried to hide a fidget.

Andrew caught Brian's hand. "Hey, Kurt, grab Brant. We've got to get around where he can see us."

"What? Why?" But his friends did not answer as they hustled Brian forward, squeezing their way urgently through the crowd. Slowly they inched past Fire's left foot until they could plainly see the throng of admiring fans worshipping Fire's penis. Their attention was obviously very pleasing to the giant. The hefty bulk was growing even larger. As Brian's friends pushed him into position, the mighty shaft began to rise up away from the crowd. They tried to follow it, standing on tiptoe, raising their hands as high as they could to continue their caresses, but inevitably it rose out of their reach and kept going, and the crowd let out a squeal of delight as the member reached its full awesome erection. Brian could feel the heat radiating from it, and even at a distance of several yards its musk was almost overpowering.

All at once Andrew shouted, "OK, now!" and he and the others began to wave the big foamcore squares that Brandt had been toting all evening. "Fire!" they shouted in unison. "Hey, Fire! Look down here! Down here!"

Somehow over the general clamor they managed to catch the giant's attention. Fire lowered his head and fixed a curious gaze on them. Brian grabbed at Brant's arm and pulled it down long enough to see that he had written "18 today!" on the sign, and he noticed Kurt and Andrew pointing gleefully in his direction. Horrified, Brian saw the big cat's eyes widen for a moment, and then narrow. Fire nodded and smiled unnervingly.

"No way! Hold it, guys!" he pleaded.

Andrew would have none of it. "Uh-oh! Look out, Brian, I think he likes yooouuuu!"

A shadow fell over him as Fire's hand approached. Brian screamed in terror and started trying to push through the crowd to escape but they turned on him, holding him in place while laughing cruelly. "Let me go! Please, let me go!" he cried, and they did, backing away abruptly and freeing Brian for all of a half second before two warm slabs of leather squeezed around his sides. He kicked wildly as he was hoisted high over the heads of the crowd, and suddenly he was being held before Fire's muzzle, the cat's breath making his raincoat flutter noisily, Brian's terrified face reflecting in each big yellow eye.

Fire smirked. A pink tongue snaked from between his lips and slithered its way up beneath Brian's raincoat. Brian let out a yelp and kicked harder while the crowd below cheered and, egged on by Andrew, started to chant his name. Fire's tongue pressed inquisitively against Brian's torso, then his thighs. One of those great yellow eyes winked at him.

Brian's breath caught in his throat. He prayed that the people below, and especially his friends, could not see what he was desperately trying to keep hidden. He was as hard as Fire was, and the cat knew it.

Down below, Kurt was holding up a sign that boldly read "JERK OFF!" It seemed to Brian's intense dismay that Fire was giving that notion some serious consideration, but instead, he surrounded Brian in a firm but surprisingly comfortable fist and rose to his full height. Slowly he stepped forward, moving with the same careful, measured tread as before, the crowd clearing a space for each footfall and then swallowing it up afterward. Ice and Sin were doing the same, all three moving toward the center of the field.

Brian squirmed anxiously and Fire's grip tightened around him. It was hard to tell if that was meant as reassurance or as a threat. The other two were soon looming over him, leering down at him like the cats who were about to eat the canary. Sin was larger than the others, and before Brian's eyes he began to grow even taller, or so it seemed until Brian realized that Fire was crouching down again.

Craning his neck, Brian stared down over the edge of Fire's hand. Sin was standing ankle-deep in the crowd, the tiny people pressed in around his feet as though the giant feline was just another spectator. The crowd was surging again, pushing back, forming two open areas now into which Fire's knees settled. His mammoth erection bobbed ponderously. The people below were barely fast enough to hoist their plastic sheeting over their heads as a bucketful of thin fluid squirted from the tip of the giant's erection and splattered down on them.

Brian's felt his stomach lurch as the hand holding him dropped abruptly, sweeping down past the enormous shaft, the crowd below waving to Brian and clapping. Fire's grip about him relaxed and Brian slid downward, falling past the warm pads and landing awkwardly on his feet. A squealing teenage girl hugged him fiercely and kissed him on the cheek. "Happy birthday!" she shrilled and the crowd cheered. Brian hardly noticed. The light had dimmed again, and this time when he looked up he saw the fur of Fire's belly stretching over him. The big cat rested on all fours now with his gigantic erection bobbing overhead, its oozing tip seeming to point straight toward Brian.

Boom, boom, and Ice's knees came down between Fire's. Boom, boom, and Sin's knees landed just ahead of the red cat's hands.

The crowd was in a frenzy, gibbering and hooting and shrieking with delight. Brian barely heard any of it through the rush of blood in his ears. Even as the crowd jostled around him he stood rock-still, gaping up at the immense organ, watching as Ice's hand closed slowly around it and squeezed another barrelful of syrup forth. His face felt as red as Fire's hide. He felt more than heard the thundering groan from above as Ice's enormous malehood bobbed behind Fire's scrotum, probed, and began to cram its way inside. The air itself pounded with the force of Fire's heartbeat: thud, thud, thud. Behind him Sin's enormous shaft vanished yard after yard into Fire's mouth. The air itself pounded with the force of Brian's heartbeat: thud, thud, thud. The gigantic body above him began to rock to and fro, the mighty testicles swinging heavily, a thick pink shaft at either end of Fire's body appearing and disappearing over and over in a colossal rhythm, the air choked with musk, Brian's bones rattling from the giant's lustful voices, his own head spinning wildly.

Brian came at the very same time that Fire did, the thick torrent crashing down on him from above and battering him down onto his back, hammering him over and over and over with the power of liquid lust. The pounding went on for what seemed like days until Fire's semen lay upon Brian like a heavy, wet blanket. His mouth was filled with it; he swallowed to keep from choking and struggled to lift his arms. He could feel the heavy cream oozing down onto his shoulders as he mopped feebly at his face, gasping for air as soon as he cleared his mouth.

Something heavy settled on his legs and then dragged rapidly upward, sweeping away the weight and letting Brian catch a welcome lungful of air. The weight swept over him again, harder this time. He felt first his raincoat and then his shirt being hoisted up and then tugged straight off of his body, his arms flopping weakly over his head. Wiping at his eyes he managed to clear them just enough to see a beachtowel-sized tongue lay upon his legs and slide up over his torso, burying his face for an alarming moment before gliding up over his brow.

Fire's teeth loomed over him, a Cheshire cat grin with the cat still attached. Brian's shirt, soaked and sticky, dangled from a fang as long as Brian's arm. Numbly he reached for it but Fire lifted his head, hoisting the shirt just out of Brian's reach. Even with the music blaring all around him, he could hear the giant's voice thundering in his ears even as he felt it in his chest. It left him trembling, not so much for the fact that the giant could speak so clearly but for what was said.

"Come back sometime without those friends of yours and you can claim this backstage," Fire purred. A big yellow eye winked and he added, "Until then, Happy Birthday!"

Dubwana the Freshman

At ninety-nine feet in height and close to four hundred tons, Dubwana Kalakonje was the largest animal ever to walk the earth. He had become an instant international celebrity after the South African government finally revealed his existence. Dozens of television programs told the story of the remarkable life he had led after being discovered in a secret Ugandan laboratory following the fall of Idi Amin Dada. They speculated endlessly as to whether the crazed dictator had found Dubwana in the wild or whether he had been created by science to serve as a terror weapon before being spirited away to a secret reserve with the fall of the regime. I had watched every program no fewer than a dozen times. I felt that I knew Dubwana better than I knew myself. Imagine how excited I was to learn that he had chosen to attend the same American university as I did.

I was still in ninth grade when the story of the amazing giant came to light and before long I had cut out a massive collage of magazine articles and pictures and pasted them to the wall of my bedroom. I loved the declassified snapshots of Dubwana as a baby from back in the Seventies, a big spotty puffball with bright blue eyes, utterly adorable even if he was as big as an elephant, but my prize was a big full-color poster of Dubwana as a teenager towering over the South African Parliament building. I think The Natural History Channel put it out as a promotion or something. In the poster, he had about him a colorful African wrap and a big fang-filled smile on his muzzle. The only part that I did not like was the logo that they had slapped onto it: Big yellow letters with black spots, an obvious play on Dubwana's cheetah-like appearance, which read "TRIUMPH OF SCIENCE OR FREAK OF NATURE?" I was often tempted to cut that part off since I didn't think of Dubwana as either one. In my mind he was a triumph of nature, a thing of such beauty and power that it made my heart race just thinking about him. I suppose I was in love even back then.

Words can't describe exactly how I felt when it was announced shortly after the beginning of my freshman year that Dubwana Kalakonje, the famous Colossus of Africa, had made arrangements to be educated at an American university: mine. The news hit me like a brick and I was punch-drunk for quite a long time after hearing it. The very idea was surreal, as though I was suddenly stuck in one of the thousands of dreams I'd had over the past few years. For a while I was even afraid to go to sleep at night, worried that I just might wake up and find that, indeed, it had all been in my head.

A year never passed more slowly for me. I am sure, though, that there were a lot of soaring blood pressures within the university's administration which had been given precious little time to prepare for the arrival of the giant. They started off with a masterful fund-raising campaign that attracted just about every major corporation in the country as well as generous input from the U.S. Government. With money in hand, they hired a New Jersey construction firm to build an immense dormitory on a tract of fallow farmland adjoining the campus. I got to watch the structure being erected, day by day something that looked like a huge barn growing up over the trees that bordered the university's land. The ground rumbled daily from trucks and earthmovers as they carved out wide roadways crisscrossing the campus from one end to the other. It gave us all a chance to grow accustomed to the constant tremors we would be feeling once the new student arrived.

Closed-circuit TV monitors and speakers were installed in almost every place that students gathered so everyone could watch the preparations being made, and I watched religiously. The Press was everywhere, constantly wandering around campus and through the dormitories, ceaselessly pestering people for their thoughts on the subject. I avoided them as much as I could. I knew from reading his biography that Dubwana was a shy creature who understood the curiosity that people held for him but was nonetheless uncomfortable with the attention that curiosity drew. I hoped that the university was also aware of this and would keep the newshounds away so that their most famous student could concentrate on his studies.

Time inched forward. The final weeks before Dubwana's arrival seemed like years; the final days seemed like weeks, and the final hours, well, those were back to feeling like years. Then, as thousands of eager students, townspeople, and cameramen gathered in the fields alongside the campus, the fresh autumn air was shaken by a deep, shuddering roar. From over the horizon there appeared a monstrous airplane, a military cargo transport, its engines straining with the enormous weight of its contents. It lumbered across the sky and headed for a special runway that had been sliced out of the rolling farmlands by the Army Corps of Engineers. A stand of trees at the far end of the field blocked our view of the landing itself, but we could all hear the engine's roar subside and then stop entirely, and we waited breathlessly.

At first we felt only a quiver, hardly noticeable at first. The crowd, which had been murmuring excitedly, fell silent. We felt it again, stronger, and then again, stronger still. A few excited whispers began to flit about. My heart was pounding so hard in my ears that I could barely hear them. The ground shook harder and harder, like a mighty drumbeat, slow and measured, drawing steadily nearer.

Like distant artillery, a dull boom began to echo around us. We felt another tremor and a pair of rounded ears appeared over the treetops in the distance. Still another tremor, and into our view appeared the spotted head of a cheetah, swaying slowly to and fro as it rose higher above the trees, its eyes cast downward. A pair of narrow shoulders shrouded in blue appeared beneath that feline head, and the crowd realized all at the same time that the newcomer was wearing a university T-shirt. The applause drowned out even the thunder of the approaching footsteps.

The great cat's lips drew back in what looked to me like a shy smile although his eyes never glanced up from the ground. Taller and taller he loomed, and then a huge leg swung over the treetops, an enormous foot, or more like a paw, crashing to the earth and raising a cloud of dust around it. There the giant paused, finally raising his eyes toward the clamoring crowd ahead. For a moment I imagined that he was looking straight at me, his gaze lingering just a second before it dropped once more. He lifted his other foot over the treeline and set it down. Boom.

Ahead of him a trio of police four-by-fours fell into formation. The giant followed slowly, clutching in his hand a suitcase that looked big enough to hold all of the people who had gathered to greet him. The impact of his feet made the police vehicles bounce visibly as they approached, the crowd parting ahead of them to make a clear path for the big cat. As he drew closer he stopped again, and his eyes flickered over the many upturned faces below him. Then, taking a deep breath, he stooped and set his suitcase down. When he spoke it was as though a sudden thunderstorm had broken out, but one with the most pleasant and musical African accent.

"My name is Dubwana Kalakonje," he boomed. A few people around me put their hands over their ears, a gesture which he must have noticed because he winced apologetically and lowered his voice. It still made the air quiver around me but it was no longer painful. "I am very much honored to have been accepted at this institution, and I am looking forward to beginning my studies."

He fidgeted a little, his tail flicking about behind him as though he were very nervous. The speech sounded as though he'd practiced it too much. "I have been asked if I would be willing to let you all see the accommodations that have been...that have been put together for me. Since some of you are curious, you are welcome to visit for a short time. I ask only that you please watch my step."

Quiet laughter rolled through the crowd, but many of them were just staring in silent awe, the joke not registering. Dubwana smiled, looking relieved to have gotten through his little speech, and gathered his suitcase back up. Policemen urged a few stragglers off of the packed dirt road and started toward the barn that would serve as Dubwana's home, with the giant following close behind. His eyes remained firmly locked on the ground ahead of him. He walked with a slow and deliberate tread as if taking great care not to step on any of his future classmates. I stood motionless with the other gawkers as Dubwana stepped right in front of me. The impact jarred my bones as his foot sank down into the rock-hard earth as easily as into wet sand. In a few seconds it rose again, dust swirling around it in graceful whorls. In just six steps he was a hundred yards down the road, with the onlookers falling eagerly in behind.

I paid only nominal attention to Dubwana's tour as he opened the doors to his house to give the spectators a peek at its interior. It was functional, if not very fancy. There was a mat on the floor for him to sleep upon – he explained that such was what he was accustomed to in his homeland – a few huge shelves, and an alcove in the back with "the necessary plumbing."

Flashbulbs flickered wildly as Dubwana began to unpack his clothing. I noticed that it consisted entirely of oversized T-shirts and shorts with the logos of his corporate sponsors emblazoned on them. That made me angry. Such indignity, to be forced to wear what were basically billboards in return for a corporation's "generosity." Why, it was nothing more than prostitution! And these people, these gaping yokels, what right had they to be there? How dare these people treat such a remarkable creature like a sideshow attraction? I wanted to rush to the front of the crowd and push them all away, send them back to their holes to find some other freak to take pictures of.

The police beat me to it, though. "...and the entire building has the most efficient sound-proofing known to modern engineering, so I hope that I will not disturb you all if I snore," Dubwana concluded. "And now, please forgive me for being a rude host, but it has been a long and cramped journey for me and I shall need to rest. I look forward to seeing you all in class."

On cue, the police began to bustle people away from the building. Dubwana smiled down at us, and once again I fancied that his gaze lingered on me for a moment before he pulled the big doors shut.

To my great relief, all of my concerns over Dubwana's privacy had not been lost on the university. An email from the president welcoming us back to campus included a bold paragraph saying that the field surrounding Dubwana's house was absolutely off-limits. It went on to describe the various punishments for being caught there, and remember that campus police are watching, and remember also that the earthen paths are for Dubwana's use only and that students found traversing them were in big trouble as well as in danger of being trampled, and blah blah blah. I was pleased that such great care had been taken to ensure that Dubwana would not be turned into a tourist attraction, but then it occurred to me that it was going to make it that much more difficult for me to talk to him. Still, I was eager to try. Sequestered though he might be, I was not going to pass up even the tiniest opportunity to meet him.

The administration had kept Dubwana's class schedule a closely guarded secret in order to prevent a run on those classes, so there was great excitement among the students on the first day of the semester as everyone wondered where the remarkable new student might be seen. Everyone was whispering and craning their necks toward the "cathouse," as the barn had been dubbed, but Dubwana had not made an appearance by the time the first classes got underway. I fretted that I might not have any classes with him since I was a year ahead. It was not uncommon for freshmen to take second-year classes if they performed well enough on placement tests, though, and Dubwana was said to be highly intelligent, so I held out hope that we still might bump into one another.

My second class of the day was an English literature course, one of those that nobody takes voluntarily other than to satisfy a Humanities requirement. Like all classes of its kind, it was held in a musty room with no windows, apparently designed to get us into the spirit of reading crumbling old tomes by candlelight. I slumped into a chair, bored, and was pondering whether the Cliffs Notes section of the bookstore would have any stock left when the professor shuffled in. "Good morning, everyone," he said with as much cheer as a doctor informing a patient of a diagnosis of syphilis. "Mr. Kalakonje, are you joining us?"

The speaker on the wall behind me crackled with a low, lyrical voice. "Yes, I am, thank you."

"Good. Now, the title of this course is, naturally, English Literature Twenty-Three, an exploration of works from the period between the War of the Roses and..."

I heard nothing past that. I just sat staring like a moron and shaking all over. It was him! He was in my class! Even if all I could see was a black box on the wall it was still Dubwana's voice. I imagined him being just on the other side of it. To me it was as though the box *was* Dubwana, sitting there right next to me. I could feel the thunder of his voice in my bones. I could almost touch him.

Somewhere along the line the class came to an end. I cannot remember a single thing the professor said except for his closing remarks. "No questions? Mr. Kalakonje, have you any questions?"

"No, I do not. Thank you."

"Dubwana!"

My voice echoed what must have been five times off the dusty walls. Everyone turned and stared. The silence that followed was, as they say, deafening, and I felt warmth rushing into my cheeks. After a moment the speaker crackled, "Yes?"

I was paralyzed. I had no idea what to say, and even less of an idea why I had suddenly blurted out his name. "I...um, I just wanted to say that it is a real pleasure...um, to have you in class with me. With *us!*"

There was another pause. "Thank you very much," the voice said politely. "It is a pleasure to be here."

That was all. Every single student in the room began to snicker. The professor was smirking. Mortified, I gathered up my books and scuttled out without another word.

I felt like an idiot, which of course I was. Once outside, I found myself a bench and plopped down on it. There were some bemused looks from classmates as they sauntered past me out of the building, although one did make a kindly effort to cheer me up. "I know how you feel," she said kindly as she walked by. It didn't make me feel any less of a jerk, but it felt good to know I wasn't alone in my admiration for the giant.

I was seriously considering blowing off my next and final class of the morning when I felt a sudden trembling in the earth, then a tense stillness, and then another quiver. I jumped up from the bench, excitement welling up in me, my earlier humiliation forgotten. Some people hurried to join me, more and more of us gathering as the pounding cadence grew louder and stronger.

Maple trees overhung the area where we had gathered, their big leaves hiding the sky from view. Near us was one of the broad dirt pathways that had been bulldozed across the campus. With each impact the dust on the pathway puffed upward in little clouds. A pair of male students, ignoring the gasps and warnings of their classmates, climbed eagerly over the rope barrier that separated us from the path. They shielded their eyes and looked skyward.

"Pardon me, please."

The words, roaring from on high like a low-flying jet, sent the two scrambling frantically back over the rope. Leaves shaken loose from the trees started to trickle down around us as the steady pounding grew more violent. Then a foot the size of cargo van descended from the canopy above. It fell hard, jarring us with a collective gasp. I could only gape in awe as the huge foot settled into the dirt, anklebone and tendons flexing beneath the fur as the unimaginable weight rolled toward the toes. Another foot swept past, whistling softly through the air, and the first one rose smoothly to follow.

"He's going to the science building," someone murmured. All at once the crowd was in pursuit, all babbling excitedly. I ran along with them through the trees and out into the open. Dubwana loomed overhead, his muscular legs flexing with each step, tail swaying behind him in a beautiful and perfect wave. I felt an almost painful stirring deep inside, a gnawing feeling which I had felt even as far back as the first time I put the pictures of Dubwana up on my walls. Back then I did not understand it; now, however, as hard as I tried, I could not ignore the yearning that was boiling up within me, could not deny any longer that Dubwana really turned me on.

He stopped outside of the science building with the crowd close at his heels. Under his arm he had a small bundle, though small only to him. He unfolded it into a mat which he spread in a hollow behind the building, and then sat down upon it and folded his legs. In his lap he placed a flat board upon which lay the largest sheets of paper that I had ever seen. Glancing past them, he seemed to notice for the first time the crowd that had gathered around him.

He looked at first pained, his ears sinking back against his head, but then they stood up again and his features softened into a patient smile. "I hope nobody will miss class on my account," he rumbled. "I would feel very guilty."

The gentle admonishment hit its mark. Awkwardly the students began to shuffle away, one at a time, until I was left standing by myself beside the immense feline. He peered at me expectantly, but I made no move. I couldn't. In my dreams I had stood in this same position with him dozens of times. Now, standing completely motionless before him, I could feel for the first time the warmth radiating from his furry hide, the puff of his breath swirling around me. My brain seemed to have disconnected itself from my body. An hour seemed to pass. Finally, mercifully, he broke the silence. "You look petrified," he said in a voice that was surprisingly quiet for his size. "I will not eat you, if that is what you are worried about."

I managed to jerk myself out of the trance. "Oh...me. Sorry! Ha-ha...I'm taking physics, uh, in here, in a minute, I mean now, so I belong here, and...I should be getting inside, I guess."

He nodded. "Yes. They are about to start." He turned to peer into one of the windows, but then his head swung back toward me. "Say..."

I stiffened.

"Aren't you in my Literature class?"

My heart fell into my belly at the sudden reminder of my mortification. "Yeah," I mumbled. "That was me. Sorry about that. I felt like such a jerk."

"Don't," he said with a soft chuckle. "It was nice to be welcomed. Now quick, get inside. They're starting without you."

"Yeah. Right. Uh, see you!" I backed away from him and then darted into the side door of the building, up the stairs, and into the classroom. I could see Dubwana's face filling the windows at the rear of the room as I entered. The professor gave me a cold look and glanced very pointedly at his watch, and then began his lecture.

I noticed that there were other people who were having as much trouble as I was concentrating on their notes. All around the room heads would occasionally turn and peek backward at the yellow slitted eyes that gazed in at us. It reminded me of a horror movie scene. All that was missing was the heroine with the bouffant hairdo letting out her piercing scream as a big furry paw reached in for her. The image would have made me laugh if my head hadn't also been filled with other images that I was trying hard to bury in my guilty imagination. They stayed with me throughout the entire class, and once again I could remember nothing of the lecture afterward.

When at last the class was dismissed I hurried outside, hoping for a chance to try to make a better second impression on Dubwana than my first, but he had already gotten up and was quite a distance away by the time I emerged from the building. I could see crowds lining the ropes as he made his way down the path toward the cathouse and eventually disappeared behind the treetops.

I tried very hard not to dwell on just how foolish I had once again made myself look.

The days plodded on as the semester got into full swing. I was surprised to find that the spectacle that Dubwana had caused with his arrival very quickly faded. In the same way that ironworkers learn to dance around on high girders without even a thought about falling, the students soon grew accustomed to the giant's presence. Reports on the news died down; after a week, very few people flocked to the path to see Dubwana pass by, and after two weeks nobody stood any more to wait for his arrival outside of the science building – nobody except for me, of course, although I tried not to be too obvious about it. I found excuses, or made them up, to just happen to be in the same places he would be. I realized that my attraction to him had become almost an obsession – all right, not just "almost." I would follow him around now and then just to watch his buns flexing under his shorts. The sight alone made me lightheaded and it was all I could do to keep from tripping over benches along the way.

The one thing that I wanted more than anything was the one thing that I could not do, and that was talk to him for any length of time. It angered me that I couldn't get over the butterflies I felt whenever I got his attention. My stomach would knot up as tightly as my tongue and the most that I could bring myself to say to him was, "Hi again," or something inane like, "It's going to be a cold one tonight." That was especially ludicrous, since the temperature in that part of the country had not dropped below sixty degrees for decades. Dubwana answered simply that he had enough fur to keep warm, and that naturally made me think about warm fur, and that made my tongue twist up so badly that I could only nod and walk away.

I kept telling myself that to obsess over him like that was not only harmful to me, but it was also disrespectful to Dubwana. Of course, the mind can rarely talk sense to other parts of the body, and three weeks into the semester my mind finally gave up the fight. I do not remember if it was anything in particular that drove me over the edge, but with thoughts of Dubwana spinning unrelentingly through my head all day long, by evening I lost all sense of rationality and decided that it was time for me to sneak in to his house to see him. The very idea was insane, of course. Four students had already been caught trying the same trick. The university had made fine examples out of them, and after that nobody else had dared to try to approach the cathouse without Dubwana's prior consent and the requisite Campus Security escort.

Nobody, that is, until that night. The risk was worth it to me. I was desperate, and as I said before, not really in my right mind. Love will do that to you.

It was late, it was dark, and there was a damp chill in the air that kept many of the students indoors. I had little trouble sneaking across the open field toward the cathouse without being spotted. Only after I had reached the shelter of the towering walls did I bother to think about how I was going to get in. There were two human-sized doors in the building, but of course both of those would be locked tight. I tried listening at them but there was nothing to hear. The soundproofing inside the building lived up to its advertising. Growing more desperate and less rational I prowled in a slow circle around the building. I rose on tiptoe as I passed the smaller barn that housed Dubwana's supply of cows – civilized though he was, he was still a predator – for fear that they would start a racket if I disturbed them. The last thing I wanted was to be caught when I was so close to my goal. What might happen afterward – well, I was not thinking of that. It did not seem to matter. After passing twice between the two structures I finally noticed a maintenance ladder attached to the cathouse wall and leading up into the darkness. It seemed like such timely good fortune that I was well on my way up before I even had a chance to think about how far away the ground was getting.

The ladder led along the curve of the roof to its peak. There I found a long, narrow platform which spanned a row of skylights stretching the full length of the building. The nearest ones were covered by drawn shades on the inside, but I could see light streaming up from one further down the rooftop. Treading carefully to avoid any creaking boards that might give me away, I snuck over to the window and peeked down into it...and was overwhelmed.

Dubwana was passing below me, the top of his head gliding past the skylight, his tail following like a giant spotted snake behind him. The building shuddered with his footfalls even though no sound escaped as he vanished into the bathroom. I waited, trembling with excitement and barely breathing, until at last he reappeared, and when he did he was naked.

I thought my heart was going to stop, or explode, or both. The sight was like a bolt of lightning going through my body. I had to bite my lip to keep from crying out in sheer delight. Dubwana stopped directly below me, lifted onto his toes and stretched, raising his enormous hands up over his head. They clenched in the air just a few inches below my perch – God, they were big up close. His body, as lean and rangy as any cheetah should be, was so smoothly muscled, so perfect. His clothes always made him look skinny; without them, I could plainly see just how much strength was housed in that slender frame. I remember thinking at that moment that I would never again in my life see a sight as enrapturing, as overpowering, as utterly arousing as the one below me.

I was wrong.

After his grand stretch he sat down and then settled back on his mat, sprawling himself out as only a cat can. Right away my eyes fixed on his groin. Guilt was the furthest thing from my mind now; there was only the sensual splendor of that giant cat stretched out below me. I held my breath as I watched his hand reach to cover the long, flaccid sheath that lay on his belly, and which quickly began to swell larger beneath the touch. Before my eyes the most enormous malehood in the world emerged, growing larger every second, crawling smoothly up along his belly and then vanishing again as his fingers surrounded it. His fist started to slide languidly along its whole length. I was hypnotized by the way its glistening surface would disappear only to emerge again on the other side of his hand. My eyes followed every inch of every stroke, drinking in the display. When the night breeze wafted past me I could feel cool moisture at the front of my pants.

Dubwana's hand abruptly jerked away from his erection. The motion was so sudden that it startled me out of my stupor, and with an icy jolt I realized that Dubwana was sitting up, eyes wide and staring straight at me. It was only then that I noticed my shadow on the glass pane before me. At some point the moon had slipped unnoticed from behind the clouds, and now it had trapped me in a glaring silhouette.

Dubwana rolled to his feet and seized a pair of shorts from the clothes rack. Snarling angrily, he scrambled into them and stamped toward the door. "Uh-oh," I said aloud, and then I, too, was scrambling. No longer worried about making noise I made a mad dash toward the ladder which was suddenly much farther away than I remembered it being. I almost made it, and was reaching for the top rung when a furry hand with claws as big as farming sickles swept up from below and crashed down inches ahead of me. The roof rocked violently with the impact. My feet skidded on the tar-paper as I tried to stop and run in the opposite direction. The hand started groping behind me, a thunderous growl rumbling from below the edge of the roof. I yelped and kicked back when I felt a finger brush my leg; a half-second later something like a warm leather blanket fell down on my back. It was unbearably heavy and drove me down to my knees. Fingers surrounded me, squeezing me into submission, and then I was being hauled violently through open air. The wild ride made my stomach twist and lurch as the lights of the university streaked by, until abruptly I was staring into the moonlit face of the giant cheetah, his teeth bared and glittering almost as ferociously as his eyes were.

"What do you think you are doing?" he demanded. I expected to be deafened by his voice, but through his clenched jaws his voice was only a frigid hiss. His fingers tightened slowly around me, making it harder and harder to breathe. "Eh? Say something. What were you doing up there?"

I wanted to squirm but I was held so firmly that I could not budge. I could not even twitch a finger, my body completely enveloped in his hand, his flesh pressing tightly inward on all sides against me. "P-please," I somehow managed to sputter. "I'm sorry. I didn't mean anything."

His grip relaxed a little and he glanced quickly from side to side in a motion that filled me with dread. I was certain that he was looking to see if there were any witnesses. It was terrifyingly obvious just then that he could kill me in a heartbeat, and his eyes burned with so much fury that I thought for certain he was about to do so. It would take only a casual tightening of his fist and I would be dead, and someone who could eat a whole cow could very easily dispose of a human body. I wondered if I would live long enough to feel any pain.

Instead, he took a very deep breath and closed his eyes for a long moment, and when he opened them again he seemed more flustered than angry. "Where do you get the right to spy on me? You have been following me around for weeks, and now you try something like this! Why won't you leave me alone?"

Those words crushed me more thoroughly than he could have with all the strength in his hand. "I'm sorry," I said shakily, my fear overcome by dismay. "I mean, I'm really sorry. I just...I just wanted to see you."

His grip tightened again, just a little. "You see me every day. I can never get away from you!" A growl rumbled in his throat. "I am going to call the campus police. I can't have people like you stalking me."

"No!" I swallowed and closed my eyes tightly. "I'll leave you alone, I promise. I really didn't mean any harm. I couldn't help it. I just had to see you. I won't come near you again."

He snorted, his breath whipping past my hair. "So what did you have to see me for?" he said bitterly. "Anxious to see the giant freak? Maybe you were going to sell tickets to see me, eh? Come see the spotted giant for only a dime, is that it?"

"No..." Tears now started flowing freely. "It's nothing like that. I swear it! I'm just...I'm attracted to you."

He fell silent and stared at me, his eyes wide in the moonlight. He shook his head briskly and then stared again. "What?"

"I'm...attracted to you," I said in a very weak voice.

Dubwana continued to stare, his ears back, and then he groaned and shook his head hard. The earth shuddered as he carried me to the front of his house, squatted down, and dumped me unceremoniously onto the path. "You will not bother me again," he snarled as he stood up again. I rolled over, staring up at him, and the sight of him made my heart freeze solid. I suddenly knew what it felt like to be a beetle about to be stepped on. That awful, blazing fury had come back to his eyes and when I saw his right foot lift from the ground I fully expected to see it come rushing down at me. Instead, he stepped back and grabbed the handle of the door. "Get out of here now. Go on!" he snapped, waving his other hand at me. "Get out! Go away and don't come near me again!"

The door crashed shut ahead of me, and then everything was agonizingly silent. I saw a yellow flashing light reflected off the wall ahead and knew that Security was coming to investigate the disturbance. Crawling to my feet, I crouched and scurried as fast as I could for the cover of the trees nearby, and from there on to my own dormitory. If they had wanted to, the security officers could easily have tracked me down by the trail of tears I left behind.

The next few days were absolutely miserable. I wanted nothing more than to apologize to Dubwana for what I had done, but he had made it abundantly clear that he wanted nothing to do with me. That alone hurt more than anything. For years I had idolized him, dreamed about him, and now that very obsession had caused me to lose it all. I found myself wishing that he *had* squashed me that night. It would have spared me the pain of living every day knowing just how badly I had screwed things up.

I avoided him as much as I could, which was hard on me. I even took to sitting with my back to a pillar in the physics lecture hall so that Dubwana would not have to see me when he looked in, and that I would not accidentally catch a glimpse of his cold, indignant eyes peering back at me. I tried to deal with it, to put him out of my life and move on, but I still cried a little when I thought of how I had managed to ruin the one thing in life that I had ever really wanted.

Another week passed, or maybe it was more. I had fallen so far behind in physics since it was so hard for me to concentrate in class that I made up my mind to drop the course entirely. After one more lecture of brooding and squirming in the glow of the unseen eyes behind the pillar, I gathered up my books as usual and slumped out through the side door which I had begun using to avoid passing the giant seated outside. I only got a few steps before my name came rumbling down at me from above.

I stopped short, almost dropping my books, and could not muster the courage to turn around. "That's your name, isn't it?" the voice boomed. I managed to turn then and peered mournfully up at

Dubwana. He was watching me, his face expressionless, his eyes felinely unreadable. "I want to talk to you for a second, if you have time."

Just standing before him was agony for me. I could think of nothing but the justifiable anger in his voice as he had driven me away from his house. Shame burned hotly behind my cheeks. Whatever he had to say, I knew that I deserved it. "Yes?" My voice was hardly more than a squeak.

He stood and folded his mat, then peered down at me for a few seconds. His tail flipped behind him. He seemed to be considering his words carefully. "I realize that I was very harsh with you last week, perhaps more so than was called for."

I shook my head in disbelief. "No, you weren't. I deserved it. What I did – God, I can't believe I was such a jerk. If someone had done that to me, I know I would have..." I made a vague, uncomfortable gesture with my hand.

"Well, yes." He touched a fingertip thoughtfully to his chin. "I'm still not very happy with having my privacy invaded." Here my heart sank painfully, but then he smiled a little. "But in thinking about it, I don't think I should have been as stern as I was. Would you please come and see me tonight? I would like to talk this over so that we will both feel better."

It was like being hit by a truck. "Tonight? You mean, as in, tonight?"

He laughed a little. "Yes, tonight, if you want to. After dinner, though. I do not think you would be happy to visit while I am eating dinner."

I thought of the cow barn next to his house. "Um. Yeah...sure. Look, I really am sorry. I feel like such a shit."

"That's good. It will keep you from doing it again." He smiled at me, then tucked his mat and his notepad under his arm and strode off down the path. "This time you can come in through the front door," he said over his shoulder. "Just remember to ring the bell first."

I did not know whether to jump for joy or crawl under a rock. Just thinking about that terrible night was painful for me, but I could not just give up the chance to apologize to him a few thousand more times. I swore to myself that I would bury the lingering memory of seeing him unclothed and pleasing himself. By some miracle I had been given another chance to get close to him, and this time I was not going to let anything in the world spoil it.

A bored security guard met me at the end of the path that led to Dubwana's house. I had expected to be marched up to the door like a prisoner on his way to the gas chamber, but the guard simply checked my ID and reminded me to follow the rope and stay off the path itself, and then he went on his way. It felt almost strange to be walking under the lights beside the path rather than stealing through the shadowy fields, after having convinced myself that the opportunity would never come around for me.

The big door loomed like a mountain over me, dwarfing the tiny man-sized door that I had first tried on the night I sneaked in. There was a doorbell beside that smaller door, and I pushed it a little apprehensively. After a tense pause there was a buzz and a click, and with a deep breath I pulled the door open and stepped inside.

Dubwana was sitting cross-legged on his sleeping mat, his notepad across his lap. A projector mounted high on one wall cast the image of a page from our physics textbook onto the wall opposite. As I closed the door behind me Dubwana glanced up, smiled, and set his work aside. With the push of a button the physics text vanished. "I am glad you came by," he said, his voice echoing sonorously in the enclosed space even though he was making an obvious effort to speak softly. "Please come closer."

I did, treading slowly and carefully in an effort to hide the shaking in my knees. Dubwana was wearing only a pair of shorts with the Exxon tiger smiling out at me from one side. His shirt lay balled on the floor nearby. I kept my eyes locked on his face and forced myself to smile. *Don't blow it*, I kept telling myself. *Keep your eyes on his. No gawking.* "Are you sure?" I said, only a little strained. "I would understand if you were still pissed at me."

"Maybe a little," he said, rubbing his chin with a finger. "But I got to thinking, if you were so eager to see me that you felt you had to sneak around like a thief in the night, then maybe I should be flattered instead of angry."

I laughed and made a little helpless gesture with my arms. "Well, what can I say?" My stomach was doing its knotting-up thing again, and my tongue was sure to follow if I did not get it under control. "Ah, is there a chair around?" I thought that if I could sit down it might help me to relax.

Dubwana's brow furrowed. "Oh!" he said as he glanced around the room. "You know, there isn't. I'm so sorry. I should have some of those brought in. I don't think about it, you see, since I don't use them."

"Oh. You mean never noticed before?"

He shook his head.

A sudden realization struck me. "Does this mean," I said uncertainly, "that I'm the first person who has visited you?"

For a few seconds he was silent. "Well, now that I think about it, yes." Something in his eyes told me that this was something he had indeed thought about, and often.

"But that's...I mean, that's unbelievable. I would've thought that people would be lining up outside." I spread my arms. "I mean, it's not like you don't have room. You could fit a whole crowd in here."

He shook his head again and dropped his gaze. He looked pained. "I don't want a crowd. I want..." He stopped and took a deep breath. "I don't think I can explain it."

"Well...you can try, maybe."

"No. It's all right. Let's talk about something else." He gave me a brave smile.

"OK," I said, "If you really want to. But if you can't talk to your stalker, who else can you talk to?"

That caught him off guard. His head twitched back and he gave me a very odd look, and then he broke into a grin and let out a roar of a laugh. "That is hard to argue with, I suppose." He shrugged helplessly and looked around the room. "Let's see...maybe you can sit here." He folded down a corner of his mat and pressed his finger on it to see if it would make an adequate seat for a guest my size.

A frequent scene that had played out in my dreams came to mind. "How about this?" I offered, holding my hand out and pointing to my palm.

"Oh, no! Believe me, it makes people very uncomfortable to have me hold them."

I smirked at him. "You already held me once. It wasn't so bad then."

He looked skeptical. "Wasn't it?"

"Well, yes, it was," I admitted. "But the second time is bound to be easier."

That made him laugh again. "I suppose, if you insist." He hesitated for a moment, and then leaned forward, lowering his hand. My heart raced. As I had so many times in my dreams, I climbed into his open palm and sat down. "Hold on," he said as his fingers curled and his palm cupped beneath me. Even though he was careful, I still felt my stomach being left behind as I was raised into the air.

Dubwana's face loomed, both yellow eyes fixed on me, so much friendlier than the last time I had seen them this close. "Are you still sure?" he said with an edge of concern in his voice.

"Oh yes!" I said too quickly, and then I gulped down my adrenaline and tried to look nonchalant. "Yes, I'm fine. Now, what was that you were saying?"

He nodded and then stared thoughtfully past me into the distance. "I have never really had many friends," he said softly. "A few teachers that I was fond of, the people who cared for me. They were my family, though. There were some boys who slipped in to play with me when I was on the reserve. They taught me so much and I loved being with them. But that was in the days of Apartheid, and one day they were caught by two of the white overseers." He swallowed, and quickly changed the subject. "So other than a very few friends, the only two kinds of people in the world to me were my teachers, and the people who only wanted something from me.

"That's how my whole life started, actually. I come from Uganda originally. I do not remember much, but they tell me that I was supposed to be a weapon of some sort for them."

I nodded. "Yes. I read all about that."

He nodded, too. "I don't think I would have made a very good weapon. Actually, it's more that I can't bear thinking of what sort of weapon I might have made. I was just a kitten then, and I suppose they could have brought me up however they wanted to, but fortunately I had a very good upbringing in South Africa. When I imagine what I might have been like if I had stayed in Uganda." He blew out his breath and looked down. "My size, you know, my strength – I don't even like to think about it."

"I understand." I had started to pet softly at his thumb, and when I realized what I was doing I quickly drew my hand back. He did not seem to notice.

"But to get back to what I was saying," he continued. "Other than my teachers, the whole world seems as though they want something from me. I cannot say that I really have any friends, even here in this country. All the people who brought me here did it only because there was something in it for them from me. They get money, they get fame, they want to be seen with me in the newspaper. Here at school, for a few days people just wanted to stare at me, and then once the novelty wore off, they hardly pay attention. I do not do anything for them now, so they do not even talk to me. I suppose some are scared, but the rest are just bored. It is very depressing." He looked straight at me. "Then there is you. You're the only one who seemed to keep trying to get my attention, even when I wasn't the big news anymore." Here he grinned broadly. If those arm-long fangs had belonged to anyone but him I think I would have died of fright. He must have seen my face drain of color because he quickly closed his mouth again. "What I am trying to say is this. Yes, I was very angry at you for staring at me through the window, but afterward I could see how hurt you were, and I thought maybe I should not have been so quick to chase you away."

I was relaxing more and more into the warmth of Dubwana's palm, the resonance of his voice making it quiver beneath me, his melodious accent like a lullaby. "Well," I said casually, "I really wanted to make friends with you. I wanted to come and talk to you, but I didn't know there was a doorbell there and I thought you would be mad if I just walked in, so I thought I'd go up on the roof and see if there was..."

The words choked me. Of course I was lying. I had not been trying to get Dubwana's attention. I had been staring at his ass. I had been gawking at the bulge in his shorts. For years I had dreamed guilty little dreams of the furry giant taking me as some sort of living sex toy, of making impossible love to him, thrilling in my fantasies to his overwhelming size and power. There was no love – it was all outrageous lust, a twisted desire for his gigantic flesh.

Remorse boiled up from deep within me, its weight making my shoulders sag. Every silent rebuke I had given to the people who treated Dubwana as a tourist attraction now came rushing back at me, impaling me on a thousand sharp barbs. Sad and lonely, Dubwana had reached out to me, and now even as he held me in his hand I could think only of using him to fulfill my desires.

He must have noticed my stricken face. "What's wrong?" he said, his ears falling back slightly.

I could not look at him. "I ought to go," I croaked. "Please put me down."

His hand wavered, but did not descend. "What's wrong?"

"Dubwana..." I began, and then covered my eyes with my hand. I felt like filth. "I'm sorry. I lied to you. I've been following you around because...because I'm attracted to you. It's just like I said. I've fantasized about you for years. When I saw you, I was...I just thought...oh, God. I'm sorry."

He was silent. I could feel his breath puffing warmly across me and knew that he had lifted me closer to his face. I put both hands over my face now, the bitter confession pouring itself out along with more than a few tears. "If I was anything close to a friend I would never have been staring in your window. I was getting off on seeing you naked, though, pure and simple. I'm not a friend, I'm a fucking pervert, and I feel like shit for it."

The warmth of his breath felt closer now. "So why are you telling me this now?"

"Because I had to. I...look, I should just go. I'm sorry. I just thought you should know the truth. I didn't want you to think you'd found a friend when all you had was some lowlife lusting after you. I couldn't live with that."

My hands were growing wetter. Finally I worked up the courage to take them away from my eyes. Dubwana's chin was resting on the heel of the hand that held me, his nose almost touching my body. I was astonished to see a bemused smile on his lips. "So at least you are honest."

I looked away. "I won't blame you for hating me."

"Oh, but I don't."

"Why not, after what I just told you?"

He hummed and blew a long breath over me through his nostrils. "Because you did tell me. I don't think you would have done that if you were as much of a lowlife as you say you are."

"It must bother you, though."

"Bother? Hmm. I suppose it confuses me more than anything. Nobody has ever been attracted to me before, at least not that I know of. I find it a little flattering."

That threw me. A small, warm spark started to twinkle in my chest. "I...you aren't mad?"

"Mad? No. As I said, it is flattering to know that you find me attractive. But it is very comforting to know that you are thoughtful enough of my feelings to tell me the truth, even though it was obviously very painful for you. I think that I would be very pleased to have someone like you for a friend."

"Really?"

He smiled, and lifted his head enough so that he could nod. "Really."

I felt a few more tears roll down my cheeks, and quickly swiped them away with the back of my hand. I managed to smile back at him. "OK," was all that I could say.

Dubwana leaned back on his other hand and raised me higher so he could gaze at me levelly. "So, now that we are friends, what shall we talk about?"

We found no end of things to discuss. He told me about Africa, of his barely-remembered life in the Ugandan military before being "liberated," as he put it, to South Africa. I told him where I had come from and some of the things I had done, all of which sounded unbearably dull to me but seemed to fascinate Dubwana, who listened eagerly to my every word. After a while I no longer noticed the tremendous size difference between us. I felt comfortable and secure in his palm, as if somehow I belonged there. "Your hand is warm," I said at one point, patting the base of one finger. "I could stay here all night."

He turned his head and loosed a cavernous yawn, big teeth gleaming. "That is nice. But my arm is getting very tired." I felt his hand moving under me, like a train starting to roll. He held his hand carefully level and let his huge torso settle back until he was lying flat on the mat. The hand holding me slowly descended like an elevator and tilted, letting me slide off onto his chest. "Better," he said, the landscape rumbling heavily under my feet.

I sat down quickly, only because my legs wouldn't hold me up any more. I was surrounded by a lush field of white fur, his chest muscles rising in powerful curves on either side of me, and ahead of me his feline face hovering, propped up by two hands behind his head. My insides fluttered. When I spoke my voice sounded like an odd croak. "Are you sure?"

"I trust you," he said simply. His chest rose softly as he inhaled, my body rising with it, and then sinking gradually back down again. I could feel the throb of his heart beneath me; it felt exactly like the shock of his footsteps when he walked. I fidgeted, but Dubwana seemed unconcerned. It was obvious, after all, that he was more than capable of fending me off if necessary.

He yawned again, and this time I could see all the way down into his throat. Then he turned and stared idly at the projector. "Physics," he sighed. "It is getting very tedious."

"Tell me about it. I don't think I've taken a single note since the class started." As I spoke there was warmth rising up from the sea of fur. The thud of his heartbeat beneath me and the gentle wave motion of his breathing were mesmerizing. My own voice sounded hollow and far away as I prattled on, enjoying the feeling of his fur sliding through my fingers as I stroked it.

Stroked? I realized with a start what I was doing and quickly tucked my hands into my lap, my face burning with embarrassment. Dubwana's whiskers flexed forward curiously. "What was that for?"

"I'm sorry!" I was saying that a lot that evening. "I didn't mean to do that."

"Do what?"

"Do...that. You know, petting you like that. It's rude and degrading."

He chuckled, jostling me on his chest so that I had to clutch his fur to keep from being rolled around. "I think it is a natural impulse to want to touch a creature that is alien to us but still fascinates us. I do not find it degrading."

"Oh," I said, still embarrassed. I put an uncertain hand down on the soft landscape beside me. "Still, I wouldn't want you to think –"

"I won't. I liked how it felt, actually."

I swallowed, my mouth uncomfortably dry. I wondered if he could feel how rapidly my heart was beating, even as I could feel his own slow and ponderous rhythm. Encouraged by his warm smile, I began to comb my fingers through the thick pelt, making furrows that I then smoothed down with my palm. "Your fur is wonderful," was all I could think to say.

"Thank you." He glanced back toward the projector. "You have not taken any notes, you say?"

"Not a one."

"Then how do you expect to pass the course?"

I shrugged. "I thought I could borrow yours."

Again I had to hold on while he chuckled. "So now the truth comes out," he said playfully. "You just want my physics notes." He yawned again, wider than ever, and closed his eyes. "Of course, you can come and see them any time."

I nodded, and nothing more was said. I continued to sweep my hand along his chest in long strokes and watched the thick fur ripple in a wave beneath my fingers. After a while one of his arms rose ponderously and passed over my head, his hand coming to rest flat on his belly behind me. I felt his breathing growing steadily deeper, the pause between them lengthening. Soon his whiskers began to twitch, and a barely audible rumbling accompanied every breath.

For a long time I just sat and watched his sleeping face. Other than the slow rise and fall of his breath his body did not move. At last I gathered my legs under me, turned, and stood up. Before me rested Dubwana's hand. Beyond that lay the flat, furry plane of his belly, and beyond that the cotton expanse of his shorts, with a long, narrow mound rising from its center. I knew that shape well from my dreams. In my mind's eye I could see myself pressed tightly against it, hugging it close to my body like a lover.

And I contented myself with the image. "I trust you," he had said.

Dubwana's hand lay motionless. Sitting down, I carefully slid my legs beneath the curve of his fingers. Dubwana made a soft muttering sound and his hand moved up and covered me, its weight pressing me warmly into his chest. It was not a lover's embrace; it was more the touch of one who had searched for something for a long time, and having found it held it close, reassuring himself every moment that it had not gone away.

I knew just how he felt. The simple warmth of that touch meant more to me than all the dreams put together.

Dubwana's Freshman Summer

"Dubwana, have you ever been in love?"

The words just slipped out one day while I was watching my giant friend clearing trees for a summer project he had undertaken. After learning the meaning of the phrase "red tape" Dubwana had finally convinced the college administration to allow him to build a jogging path to keep himself in shape. For weeks he spent an hour each day on his knees, tearing trees out of the ground with his bare hands like he was weeding a tulip bed. With nothing better to do – and eager for any excuse I could find to ogle him – I went along every afternoon and sat with him as he worked. My question, which came out of nowhere, took him by surprise. He paused and gazed down at me with an odd expression. "In love? Me?" Straightening his back, he touched a finger to his muzzle and looked thoughtful for a moment. "No, I don't believe I have," he said.

I nodded quietly and watched as he pulled up two more trees, stripped them of their branches with a swipe of his fingers, and laid them neatly in a row for the trucks from the paper mill to collect later. "I guess it was a dumb question," I said, embarrassed to have even asked it aloud. "It's kind of hard to find someone, you know, like you, I guess. Maybe a personal ad would work. 'Single male, African heritage, 100 feet tall, spots and tail, enjoys running and gardening...'"

Dubwana laughed. "That's not such a bad idea. Who knows? Maybe someone would answer." His biceps bulged as he ripped another tree from the ground. "It would be nice if there was someone else like me," he said wistfully, then added "but it wouldn't have to be. Love is in the heart, after all, isn't it?" "I am sure that my heart will know when it is in love."

"Yes," I said simply. *How right you are.*

He gripped one last tree trunk and wrenched it upward, carefully shaking the soil from its roots before piling it with the others. "There. That's the last one. How does it look?"

I turned and peered through the woods along a straight and seemingly endless scar pitted with craters and sprinkled with fresh dirt. "It looks like a bombed-out runway. I think you're a better gardener than you are an engineer."

"But which of us got the better grade in physics?" he teased, rising to his feet. "It will pack down flat once I have used it a few times."

"I'll bet. All this work for a jogging track, though — couldn't you just build a treadmill?"

Dubwana shook his head. "What good is a treadmill? I would never feel the ground under my feet or the wind in my fur. If you were a cheetah you would understand."

I lowered my voice. "If I was a cheetah..." I mumbled, letting my eyes play over the spots, big as manhole covers, on the outsides of his legs.

"What was that?"

"Nothing. So come on. Let's see how this engineering marvel of yours works."

Smirking, Dubwana rose up onto his toes, stretched his arms high over his head and then swept them downward, bending nimbly to press his palms flat to the ground. "Of course. But before we do, I want you to promise to stay at the very end of the path," He slid his palms slowly back between his feet as he spoke, stretching his mountainous, lanky form in a way that only a cat could. "We don't want you getting underfoot."

"Oh, yes, thank you for the reminder. I was just going to stand in the road and let you trample me, but now that you mention it I think I'll try survival today..."

The tip of his tail caught me from behind, just hard enough to make me stumble forward. "And no sarcasm either," he grunted.

"Can't I just ride on your shoulder?"

"No. I don't want to risk you getting hurt. I'm going to be moving quite fast." He stood up straight again and pointed a finger at me. "Now stay where I can see you, hm? No games."

Pouting playfully, I shuffled past his feet and took up a position at the end of the path. With his back turned to me he could not see me admiring the shape of his rear through his running shorts. It was a quite a breathtaking sight, one that I never grew tired of, even though it was getting harder and harder to be surreptitious about it.

Dubwana already knew that I found him attractive but we had never spoken of it since I had let it slip months before, and I worried that it might lead to some awkward moments if he were ever to catch me staring. I cannot deny that I found him sexier than hell, but there was so much more to it than that. The emotions that I hid from this bizarre and wonderful titan were so heavy that I often felt as though Dubwana himself were sitting on me. How exactly do you say "I love you" to someone fifteen times your size? It was fun to dream about – and dream I did, almost constantly – but the thought of what Dubwana might say if he knew how I thought about him was enough to keep my mouth shut. We were friends, yes, but it was ludicrous to think that I could be anything more than that. Considering his size, I could never realistically be much more than a pet to him. Love would be a joke, or at least that is how the rational part of me tried to soothe the ache in my heart. The problem with hearts is that they never listen to rational arguments.

In a flash he was off. I was buffeted by a great rush of air that blew my hair into my face as Dubwana's gigantic body suddenly lunged forward. His tail stretched out straight behind him, his mighty legs pumping so fast that they became a blur, and within two seconds he had covered half the distance back to campus. I had never seen Dubwana run before and was astonished that a creature so large could move with such speed. I could only stand there staring after his immense form as it shrank into the distance. My ears rang, but not from the sound of thunderous footfalls; rather, it was from the very shocking silence that Dubwana left in his wake. I had anticipated that he would be setting off seismographs for a hundred miles but his feet hardly seemed to be hitting the ground. The earth barely moved beneath me as he sped toward campus, the air behind him swirling into a twin vortex that whipped the trees on either side.

I watched him skid to a halt far away, a cloud of dust kicking up around his feet, and then he spun about and started back. His body grew steadily larger as he approached, an enormous spotted missile, his head lowered and ears tucked sleekly against his skull. I felt myself tensing as he loomed closer. I trusted him implicitly, of course, yet there is still a certain visceral response to having such a gigantic creature bearing down on you like that. He must have noticed my discomfort and flashed me a reassuring grin before he slapped a foot down ahead of me, pivoting upon it and plowing up a great mound of dirt as he ground to a halt. Instantly he spun around. The black pads of his toes flashed up and back over my head as he charged off, his tail following behind him in a perfectly straight line.

As I stared after him I was quaking, breathless, mesmerized by the grace and power he was demonstrating. He was in his element now. Every movement was perfect, his muscles flowing beneath his hide like a restless river. It was like watching him in a dream, this giant, this veritable god that had graced me with his companionship. The sight nearly brought tears to my eyes. He was magnificent, he was beautiful, and at that moment I wanted him more than ever before.

After ten laps along his track he slowed to a less dramatic stop at my end, his teeth gleaming in an elated smile. "Wonderful!" he purred. "Oh, I wish they would have allowed me to make it longer. Still, I should be grateful to be able to run at all." He drew a deep breath and grinned brightly down at me. "Maybe I should try out for the track team, don't you think?"

I hid the tears and brushed the longing from my eyes before he noticed either. "I'm sure you'd crush the competition."

He snickered, then bent down and offered a hand to me. "I think we've both earned a rest. You must be awfully tired from all that standing around and watching me run."

"You have no idea," I mumbled as I climbed into his palm.

Back at the oversized barn that served as his dormitory, Dubwana settled himself comfortably on the floor and lowered his hand so that I could slide out onto his lap. It was a position we often shared when we were studying. Ordinarily I would have just quietly enjoyed the closeness in secret, but this time I could barely sit still. Seeing him run, such an awesome demonstration of his elegance and strength, had fueled my desires to a nearly unbearable degree. I was keenly aware of the firmness of the great furry thigh beneath me, and more than ever before of the outline in Dubwana's shorts that lay so tantalizingly close. I nodded distractedly as Dubwana went on about the joys of the African plains. "Miles of flat land, absolutely perfect for running," he said wistfully. "I used to be able to run for hours in any direction I chose."

"I can imagine." It was getting hotter in the room. I fidgeted on his leg, trying to think distracting thoughts, but before I realized it I had blurted out, "Do you ever feel lonely?"

Caught off guard by the question, he stared down at me for several seconds before answering. "Er...well, yes. That is, I used to, until we got to be friends. I don't think I ever said thank you for that. It is difficult being the new kid."

"Hey, what are friends for?" I said quickly and patted his leg as nonchalantly as I could manage. My heart was fluttering madly. I do not believe that I had any idea at that moment what I was about to do. It all happened by instinct. Watching him run had sparked something in me, and that something had taken complete control. I was just going along for the ride at that point. "What I mean, though, is...do you ever get lonely? I mean, for physical companionship?"

He pursed his lips, his faraway expression answering more clearly than his words. "Physical? Well...I don't know, really. I don't have a lot of experience in that sort of thing. It would...well, being the only one, it is difficult...you see?"

I barely realized that I was sliding forward to the inside of his thigh. As he tried to explain further I slid down and dropped to the floor. I had started to sweat, and was probably terrified but was too lost in the moment to know it. I could feel the power in his thigh as I leaned back against it. "So what would you look for?"

"Look for where?"

"You know."

He reached up to paw at an ear. "I don't know, really," he said at last. "I never really thought of it. I suppose I would want someone who wasn't selfish, who was willing to love me for what I am. It would have to be someone I could talk to with my heart and not have to hide anything."

I listened to his words as he spoke but did not really hear them, turning my head to peer along his thigh to the point where it entered the great cloth tunnel of his shorts. Seated as he was with his legs folded the fabric bowed outward and afforded me a rare and electrifying view. In the shadows within I could see the enormous furry sheath that housed the giant's malehood. I had caught sight of it a few times in the past in spite of Dubwana's modesty. Those precious glimpses had always been from a distance, tantalizing hints of the enormity within that had fueled many a happy dream. "So if... there was someone who really liked you and wanted very much to please you, and you trusted them..."

"I imagine so. It's hard to guess. Like I said, I do not have much experience."

I had never been so close to him, not that part of him at least. I breathed in his scent and grew lightheaded. His words seemed to fade into a muffled rumble like far-distant thunder. That mammoth sheath, bigger than I was, loomed just a few feet away. Without reaching very far I could have laid my hand upon it.

And just then, I did.

Dubwana's voice caught in his throat. I could feel his incredulous gaze on me from high above. The air felt like crystal. There was a long silence, and then he whispered "Wh-what are you doing?"

My stomach knotted. I wanted to jerk my hand back and tell him I was sorry but I felt paralyzed. The flushing in my face spread throughout my body in a tingling wave that made me feel faint. His sheath was so warm, and I thought that I could feel it move ever so slightly beneath my hand. I began to caress it, brushing my shaking fingers across the thin fur. "Do you want me to stop?" I said in a voice so soft that even I could barely hear it.

Dubwana mewled and started to stammer words that died on his lips, and then he was quiet for a moment, and then in a voice that was as soft as mine he said, "No."

My head spun. Relief and elation crashed together inside of me. I had to lean against his thigh to keep from falling over. I could feel him trembling, almost as much as I was. Encouraged, I inched my way closer to his groin, my arm exploring the length of his sheath as my shoulder pushed back the fabric of his shorts, until I found myself pressed up against the delightful warmth of his scrotum. His scent, thick and masculine, surrounded me, filled every inch of me. I ducked my head beneath the hem of his shorts and for the first time, after so many months of dreaming and yearning, I laid my cheek against his malehood and let it rest there. After a moment I felt hesitant fingers upon my back, gently pressing me into the warm fluff of his groin.

For a long time he simply held me there, his thumb quivering as it rose to stroke tenderly at my head. "Earlier," he whispered hoarsely, "when we were outside, and you asked..."

"Yes. I've been wanting to do this for a long, long time."

He swallowed audibly. "I don't know. It feels good, but I'm so afraid I'll hurt you."

"I'll be all right."

Dubwana mewed quietly, and then I felt his fingers gently pinching me around the middle and easing me back away from his groin. My heart sank as for a moment I thought he wanted to stop, but when I looked up I saw neither reproach nor apology in his face. He had averted his eyes and was chewing his lip, uncertain. "Are you sure?" he said, unconsciously sweeping his tongue over his whiskers.

"I'm sure. I want to. I have ever since I met you."

One of his ears flicked and he swallowed, then he turned his head and stared at the floor beside him for a long time. Eventually he released me. I stepped back as slowly he rose to his feet and, even more slowly, he hooked his thumbs in the waistband of his shorts and slid them downward. There was a long hiss and a crackle of static electricity as the cloth dragged over his furry thighs. One foot rose before me and then thudded back down; the other did the same, and the shorts fell limply to the floor nearby. Dubwana stood over me, naked and beautiful, smiling awkwardly down at me past the pink bulk of his penis which had already begun to show from its furry housing. "I've never..." he stammered, "I mean, not with anyone, let alone someone...well, like you...I mean, I never even thought someone might..."

I smiled and held up my hand, silencing him. "I understand. It's all right."

His smile wavered a little but soon returned, and without another word he sank into a crouch, then settled carefully back to his rump. His feet swept past me and his legs landed with meaty thuds on either side. I had seen this happen in my dreams for years and devoured the sight, letting it burn into my memory forever. It took a tremendous effort to keep myself from rushing forward and throwing myself upon him. No, this was a moment to be cherished. I took my time in removing my clothing, and then I wandered slowly along the furry canyon of his legs, my arms outstretched, brushing the fur with my fingers until I stood before the huge white bulk that loomed before me. His penis was rapidly growing larger. It swung briefly sideways over my head before sweeping up and standing tall. Its surface pulsated with life and with need. Drawing in a deep breath and filling my lungs with his musk, I slipped my arms around his immense scrotum and hugged it to my body, rocking side to side to caress it with my flesh.

His thighs tensed around me. The base of his erection throbbed as the great organ jerked, bumping heavily against his belly. "Oh...that... that feels nice," he whimpered.

Smiling, I leaned back so that I could see his face past the towering organ. "Relax," I said softly. "Let me do the work."

Dubwana licked his lips again and shifted his gaze nervously, but nodded. His face disappeared from view as he laid back, his hips rocking upward and lifting his scrotum several feet off of the floor. I took a few moments to play with the giant orbs, pressing myself into the white blanket that contained them and nudging them as best I could out to the sides just to admire their weight. Dubwana mewled happily and now and then his thighs would tense, his toes curling tightly at the far end of his legs. He breathed deeply and whispered my name once, then twice.

It was time. Gripping the fur of his leg tightly with my hands I vaulted up as hard as I could, pulling downward to drag myself up onto his thigh.

"OW!" The leg jerked violently, sending me sliding awkwardly back to the floor. A few strands of fur were still clutched in my fists.

"Oh, shit. Oh, Dubwana, I'm sorry..."

"No, no!" His voice had grown huskier. A padded hand came down behind me and scooped under my rear, helping to lift me to the top of his leg. "Don't worry about it. Just...keep going. Please. Don't stop. "

I smiled, relieved, and gave his thumb an apologetic pat. Once safely atop his leg I paused once again to admire him. His body stretched before me, a vast plain of fur and muscle, and that superb erection lying so eager and inviting before my eyes was the living embodiment of so many yearning dreams. It was all I could do to keep my knees from giving out as I shuffled toward the mighty organ.

Its size was unbelievable, longer than I was tall, bigger around than three of me would have been. Warmth radiated off of it in waves. In the distance the white hill of his chest rose and fell deeply, its rhythm increasing as I threw one leg over his massive shaft and then lay the full length of my body upon it. I could feel his heart pounding through his flesh, my own pulse feeling so pitiful and insignificant against it. My arms could not encircle him fully even though I stretched as far as I could. Hugging tightly, I pulled myself up until my chin passed his flared glans and I could look down upon a crevice that looked capable of swallowing my whole head. It was already leaking a thin, syrupy fluid, and I lowered my face to grace it with a slow and loving lick.

Dubwana grunted and I was launched violently into the air. I flipped over twice before I landed hard on his belly, his erection thudding down loudly beside me. "S-sorry!" he panted, raising his head. "Are you hurt?"

"It's OK! Really. Just relax." Rolling to my knees I blinked the confusion out of my eyes, then leaned forward and stroked my fingers experimentally across the tip of his penis, watching closely as they smeared his fluid over the tender flesh. He grunted again and the gigantic organ jerked upward with tremendous force, quivering turgidly for a breathless second before crashing back to his belly. I realized with more than a little disappointment that the slightest touch upon that tender spot would turn things into a ride on a mechanical bull.

Determined, however, I hauled myself to my feet and climbed atop the great organ once more, wrapping my arms around it as far as I could behind the flare to keep myself well away from the tip. I wrapped my legs around as well, and after taking a few deep breaths, I began to pump my body up and down. Dubwana responded right away with a low, thunderous moan and his legs began to twitch. One arm rose, the forearm draping over his eyes, and he moaned again, louder this time. His reaction encouraged me and I pulled harder, grunting with the effort. My bare skin clung to his and stretched it fore and aft, dragging it up and down over the firmness beneath.

I counted twenty strokes. Dubwana's groans were now a near-continuous roar, his furry chest heaving ahead of me. His heartbeat pounded beneath my body as though it would explode out through his flesh. A dull ache began to throb in my arms and lower back, but I was set on pleasing him and redoubled my efforts.

I counted thirty strokes. Fire kindled in my muscles and gnawed at my strength. My arms started to shudder with the effort and black spots were dancing before my eyes from breathing so hard.

Thirty-five strokes. I couldn't see. My arms were burning up. My rhythm faltered, and two strokes later it ceased entirely. I lay exhausted upon his erection, gasping, my strength entirely spent.

Dubwana yowled piteously. "Don't stop now!" he pleaded.

I could hardly muster enough breath to speak. "Can't," I choked. "Totally...beat..."

"But I..." He grunted, fidgeting. "I'm so close..."

I made a valiant effort to finish him but my arms could not manage even one more stroke before they gave out. "I can't," I whimpered. "Use...use your hand. Help me. I'll be fine."

He made a soft, uncertain sound in his throat, but a needful shiver coursed through his body and helped him make up his mind. His hand rose into view and then settled gingerly upon my back. "Like this?" he mewled.

"Yes...go on...just be careful."

He nodded briskly. The pressure increased on my back as his fingers closed around both my body and his erection. Slowly he dragged me upward. I had just enough strength left in my arms to maintain my grip around him, and he gasped raggedly. "That's it," I said breathlessly, trying to sound encouraging. "That's good. Just like that."

Dubwana swallowed audibly and slid me carefully back down, and then up, and then down. Soon he was groaning again, and I was, too. My own hips were pressed tightly against the gigantic shaft, and as he stroked me against himself I was enjoying the full benefit of the motion. I started to squirm as my own desire soared, and in response Dubwana began to rub faster. The growing warmth of his erection penetrated into my bones; the heady scent of his arousal filled my head. I could not take a breath without breathing him in. Lust burned behind my cheeks and rose like a flame in my loins as my body tensed and shuddered, and moisture began to smear between my belly and the mighty shaft.

That tiny wetness, however, was not enough to ease my passage over his length as Dubwana scrubbed me harder and harder. I tried to catch my breath but could not; he was squeezing me, making me wheeze as the pressure mounted. "Um...Dubwana...." I gasped with some concern.

He did not hear me. His lustful moans were echoing off of the high ceiling of the barn. His hand was speeding up and his fist was closing relentlessly tighter. "D- Dubwana...?"

My skin was now being pulled painfully up and down as it dragged upon his. It soon felt as though it would be pulled right off. My head jerked to and fro with the force of his stroking, the rhythm becoming unbearable, as was the immense pressure as his fist clenched, threatening to crush me to pulp against his shaft. My head swam and through the sparks that danced before my eyes I saw images of that same hand gripping the trunks of stout trees earlier in the day, the wood splintering and bursting as he wrenched them from the ground.

"DUBWANA!"

The violent ride came to an abrupt halt, my head snapping forward against the rim of his glans. Dubwana growled and hastily lifted his hand and scooped me safely off onto his belly. "Can't stop...!" he hissed through clenched teeth. His fist eagerly resumed its motion without my frail body there to impede it.

My skin burned from the abuse it had suffered and my ribs ached. The disappointment was devastating, but I was not about to let every one of my dreams be dashed that evening. There was one more, and I had only seconds left to capture it. Painfully I struggled to all fours while Dubwana's titanic frame began to tense up. Muscles swelled and grew hard beneath his fur and his breathing broke into harsh gasps. He was close, now, very close. Frantically I clawed my way across his belly and knelt before the tip of his penis, which bobbed and jerked just inches away from me as his fist flew along his length. Like a worshipper before a god I rose to my knees and threw my arms out wide to accept his blessing. "Come on me!" I begged.

And he did. In my imagination I had knelt on that very spot a thousand times to bathe in the gentle flood as his warm pleasure surged over my body like an ocean wave, but what hit me at that moment felt more like a wrecking ball. A torrent of thick, gooey cream crashed into me with enough force to blast me back five feet and knock the wind out of me. The next burst felt like a linebacker had just jumped with both feet onto my stomach. I tried to sit up but was hit again square in the face. It made me see stars. The impact threw me flat on my back. It was like having one of those lead blankets the dentist uses when he takes your X-ray on top of me – no, more like six of them all piled on me at once. I could not lift my arms, could not even raise my head to catch a breath. My eyes burned when I tried to open them and they clamped themselves tightly shut again. When I tried to breathe I gulped down a huge salty mouthful that made me gag, and as I choked on it I only got more of it into my throat. I wanted to thrash; I was drowning, but couldn't move, mired like a bug in amber.

From somewhere far away I heard Dubwana call my name, and then I was being lifted into the air and flung about. Consciousness was just fading away when something swiped harshly across my face, allowing me to gasp in just enough air to cough up a lungful of semen. My face was swiped again by something huge and rough and painfully raspy. "Oww!" I bawled. "Don't do that! OW! Not the tongue!"

Dubwana's voice was agonized. "I'm sorry!" he wailed. "I'm so sorry. Please don't die!" He tried to lick me again, almost pulling off my skin.

I yelped and pushed his tongue away. "Stop! Just...just...ow! Just... get me a towel, or...a washcloth, something." His hand lurched under me, making me fall over, and a moment later an enormous tarp was draped over me. I seized it quickly and began feverishly mopping the smothering cream from my arms and shoulders. "Oh, cripes...my eyes. I can't see. I...hey!" The tarp was sticking to my skin, the cream having turned in a very few seconds into a particularly efficient glue. The more I fought to escape, the more the cloth wrapped around me, clinging to me like flypaper. "Dubwana, help!"

"What do I do?" His voice was frantic. "I can't pull it off without hurting you..."

I moaned helplessly. "Jesus. Water – take me into the bathroom, quick." The glue was becoming crusty, crackling with every movement I made and pulling at my skin in all directions. My eyes were stuck firmly shut. "Hurry!"

I was jostled all about and the next thing I knew, warm water was gushing down over me. Thankfully, Dubwana had the presence of mind to turn the valve on to a gentle trickle or else I almost certainly would have been washed off of his hand and straight down the drain. I scrubbed desperately at my arms as the crust turned first into soap, and then into gelatin before finally peeling away. At last I was able to open my eyes, although they continued to sting something terrible even after I had rinsed them for several minutes.

Dubwana was devastated. "I'm sorry," he whimpered over and over again, "I'm so sorry! This is all my fault." He looked like he wanted to die.

I stepped out from under the water and swiped the still slimy-feeling water from my arms, and then shook out my hair. "No it wasn't," I grumbled.

"I shouldn't have let you."

"It was my idea, damn it!" I snapped, and immediately regretted it. Dubwana's ears tucked back and he hung his head and a big tear rolled down along the dark stripe on his cheek. "I'm sorry," I said, but those words sounded far too feeble after such an outburst. I wanted to cry, myself. "Come on," I said more gently. Lift me up closer."

Dubwana hesitated, and then raised his hand to bring me to his face. He looked away, however, reluctant to look me in the eye. Gently I laid my hands on his cheek. Another tear trickled down over my fingers. "Hey," I said earnestly, and managed to smile. "I'm sorry. Don't feel bad. I'm still in one piece, see?"

"No thanks to me."

"Well, no," I said weakly, "but...well, you did give me what I asked for.

He sighed. "I'm so sorry that I disappointed you."

"You didn't. I mean, if anything, I disappointed me. I'd been wanting to do that with you for so long. It just...I guess I never really thought it through all the way. Physics...it never was my best subject, you know." I mustered a broader smile. "It sure was fun trying though, wasn't it?"

Dubwana shrugged, and sat down slowly. A few more minutes passed before he was able to meet my gaze. We stared at each other for a while, and then the ghost of a smile twitched at the corner of his muzzle. "Well...I always heard it said that sex spoils a relationship."

"Drowning your partner kind of has that effect."

We stared at one another for several seconds. His smile broadened slowly; mine did, too, and ultimately we burst out with uncontrollable laughter. It made my bruised ribs ache but I couldn't help myself. Dubwana had to cup his hand to his chest to keep from dropping me as he cackled. "So that's why you were spying on me back when I first arrived, is it?"

I slumped against his thumb, still chuckling. "Yeah, guilty. Hey, all I wanted was some pussy."

We laughed harder. "You little slut!" he said, raising me to his face and bumping me playfully with his nose until I fell back against his fingers. His laughter faded to a warm smile. "But I'm glad you did, anyway." He touched his nose to me more gently. "Are you sure you're all right?"

"Yes," I said, reaching to pet the side of his muzzle. "A little sore maybe, but...well, no regrets."

He smiled and blew a warm breath from his nostrils across my chest. "No regrets? You don't mean to tell me that you'd want to try that again."

"That?" I winced and rubbed the side of my chest. "Well, no, not quite that. But you know what they say: if at first you don't succeed..."

Dubwana's muzzle broke into a smile and he gave me another soft nose-bump. "We would have to be a lot more careful next time."

"Oh, definitely. I want to live to enjoy the afterglow."

A finger curled down to give me a good-natured thump on the head. "You're incorrigible." Sighing, he rested his shoulders back against the wall and lowered me down to cuddle me against his massive chest. "Well, if nothing else, I can say something now that I never really had the courage to say before."

"And that is...?"

He lowered his head, his yellow eyes glowing warmly upon me, and purred, "I love you."

An Afternoon at Number Twenty-One

Chris did not immediately see what hit him, his belly taking the full force of the impact the very moment he opened the door. The blow sent him staggering backward, gasping for breath. His feet tangled in something and he fell, landing hard on the floor in the middle of the hallway. It took a moment before he was able to focus again and he stared upward in stunned horror at his assailant.

Blazing red eyes glared above a sneering muzzle filled with fangs. The setting sunlight cast in silhouette a powerful figure sheathed in dull green scales. The creature filled his doorway, its head brushing the lintel even though it stood crouched. It took a deliberate step forward, the murderous talons on its feet scratching noisily upon the floor. Its nimble tail disentangled itself from Chris's legs and slithered to the door, which it quietly pushed shut behind the intruder.

Chris struggled to breathe and squirmed frantically backward. He tried to call for help but the blow had knocked the wind from him and all that he could muster was a croak. The effort alone seemed to enrage the creature and it bounded toward him. One of its massive feet stamped down on Chris's chest, driving what little breath remained out of his lungs. The cruel talons pressed downward as the beast curled its toes which Chris realized could spear clean through him with the barest twitch of a muscle.

"Sssilence," it rasped.

Chris stopped his struggling and stared upward in mute terror. The creature's leg towered over him like a building, and beyond it, the smoldering, slitted eyes peered down at him like scornful red lanterns. "D-don't hurt me," he squeaked.

The creature said nothing but its grin widened, and the foot on Chris's chest pressed down harder, the sharp talons pricking into his shoulders. He wheezed and grimaced, staring pleadingly up at his assailant. "What do you want?" he whimpered.

"You."

The response horrified him. Chris gulped and peered into the creature's eyes in a silent plea for an explanation, but no answer could be found in them. They were cold, reptilian, the only sign of emotion reflected in that predatory grin. "What are you?" Chris said at last, his voice small and terrified.

The monster chuckled softly. Its eyes burned brighter, paralyzing Chris in their glare. "I am Rang," it hissed. "And you are mine."

The heavy foot rose suddenly from his chest, permitting Chris a single feeble gasp of air. The creature, Rang, stooped and seized him by the arm, hauling him off of the floor. It stood tall, its horns scratching grooves in the high ceiling, and gripping him about the waist with both hands it lifted him like a doll and held him frighteningly close to its fangs. "You will be sssilent," it hissed.

Chris kicked helplessly in its grip and tried to shy away from the vicious teeth. "Please, just tell me what you w-"

Blindingly fast, the creature's left hand released Chris's waist and clamped into a tight fist around his head. A powerful squeeze sent waves of pain through Chris's skull which felt as though it might burst from the pressure.

"SSSILENT!" Rang roared and gradually released its grip. Chris whimpered and nodded, panting. Whatever this creature, this Rang, was, it was clear that the only hope Chris had to survive was to obey. After all, it could easily have killed him by now if that was all it had wanted.

Then again, there was no way of telling when it would want to.

Chris felt himself falling as Rang abruptly released its grip. He landed awkwardly on his feet and stumbled backward. Something caught him – the creature's tail. He felt it pressing against his shoulder blades, trapping him, nudging him forward. He was trembling violently and almost asked the creature again what it wanted with him, but the lingering ache in his skull reminded him that to try to speak again would be an agonizing mistake.

Rang settled down slowly to its haunches, its featureless eyes regarding Chris dispassionately. They studied him, slowly moving from his brow to his toes and back. Rang reached forward and seized his arm again. Its tail wrapped firmly around his waist, and with its other hand it gripped the front of Chris's shirt and ripped it away with a powerful yank.

"Hey!" No sooner had he uttered the word than Rang flung his shirt aside and jabbed a sharp talon into Chris's belly. Rang's teeth drew back in a snarl as its finger pressed forward, the pain increasing steadily. Chris saw himself about to be gutted like a fish, and biting back a yelp he pursed his lips and nodded feverishly.

Smirking, Rang withdrew its finger and released its grip on Chris's arm. With its tail still looped tight around Chris's waist it gripped the shivering man's pants in both hands and tore them from his body. With an evil chuckle it flicked a few stray shreds of cloth away, leaving Chris naked and vulnerable, before rising again to its full immense height.

Chris cowered as Rang towered over him. The beast stooped, its hands sweeping behind Chris's back, encircling his body and hoisting him into the air. Rang pressed him tightly against the smooth scales of its chest and wrapped its powerful arms around him. Something flicked at his forehead and when Chris looked up, he was met by the ghastly gleam of finger-long fangs barely inches away.

Rang's jaws parted and a slender, forked tongue emerged, thrusting itself unceremoniously into the startled man's mouth. Eyes bulging, Chris's first impulse was to bite down and indeed his jaw was beginning to tense when he saw Rang's eyes narrow warningly. As much as some part of Chris wanted to defy the brute, the rest of him wanted very much to survive and overruled the decision. He let his body go limp and submitted, allowing Rang's tongue to slither disgustingly into his mouth, the creature's scaly lips drawing closer and finally meeting with Chris's own.

Struggling not to gag, Chris became aware of warmth against his leg, then of moisture, then of something growing and throbbing between his body and Rang's. The beast's hips began to thrust obscenely against him. Realizing what was happening Chris grunted and tried to twist away, kicking hard until a talon poked warningly against his left kidney. Whimpering, Chris squeezed his eyes shut and tried to concentrate on remaining limp and motionless as the monster grew increasingly aroused. It was clear now what Rang wanted, and equally clear that he would tolerate no disobedience.

After several agonizing moments Chris felt his body sliding down over the rough scales. Rang let Chris's feet settle slowly to the floor. A heavy hand came down on Chris's head and pushed down hard, forcing Chris painfully to his knees. Thick fingers clenched around his skull and pulled his head forward, guiding his face relentlessly toward the towering spire of flesh that jutted forth from the beast's groin.

"Sssuck..." Rang demanded.

Chris could take no more. With a defiant yell he lashed out blindly with his hands to push the massive organ away, his body twisting hard in an effort to squirm free. Rang growled thunderously and once more his enormous hand began to squeeze excruciatingly around Chris's head. Fighting back tears of pain, Chris gritted his teeth and snarled, "No! You can't make me do this."

"Sssuck...!" The voice was louder now, threatening.

"No!" Chris's vision grew foggy and his breathing became labored. He was certain that he felt a crack somewhere deep in his skull but he was determined not to give the beast the satisfaction it demanded.

To his surprise the pressure abated. With Rang still gripping his head Chris could see only the giant's meaty thighs and the colossal erection that twitched in his face. There was a scraping sound as Rang reached for the heavy wooden hatstand that stood beside the door and dragged it closer. Gripping it in his opposite hand he lowered it down and thrust its top in front of Chris's face to give him a good look before lifting it up and out of sight. There followed a loud crack and a noisy splintering. Again the hatstand was lowered for Chris to observe. It had been bitten clean through.

There was a crash as the hatstand was flung against the wall. Silence followed, and then another command, this one low and guttural, with a strong sense of finality about it. "Sssuck!"

The pressure of the fingers around his head began to increase again and Chris feared that Rang's patience would last no longer. The heavy penis nudged insistently at his lips. Choking back a sob Chris surrendered, opening his mouth as wide as he could to allow the tip of the mighty organ to be crammed inside.

His jaw ached from the strain. Rang pushed down harder on Chris's head and the great bulk pressed relentlessly into Chris's throat, gagging him. Desperately he wrapped both hands around the middle of the shaft in the faint hope of placating the creature before it choked him to death. Rang responded immediately, his growl softening to a melodious crooning, and he rewarded the submission by pressing down less firmly on Chris's head. Relieved, Chris began to stroke with his hands, feeling the smooth, moist length sliding through his fists. He could move his head a little now and began to suckle obediently, his tongue swirling along the underside of the heavy glans. The hope that Rang would release him once he was finished spurred Chris onward and helped him set aside his revulsion. The faster he worked, the faster the monster would be satisfied and release him, or so he hoped.

Something brushed against the inside of his thigh and then slid along his groin. Chris could not see but he could tell that it was the tip of Rang's tail. Showing the same agility as when it had reached out to trip him, it now coiled around Chris's own penis like some obscene serpent and began to squeeze softly, its length rippling. Chris shuddered and tried to ignore the tingle of pleasure that shot through his loins from the unearthly touch. His own body betrayed him, his member rapidly swelling within the coils of Rang's tail in spite of the terror. Within moments Chris was fully erect and his hips had begun thrusting into the tail's embrace as though his body had taken on a mind of its own.

Dismayed at his own lack of control, Chris clenched his eyes shut and concentrated as hard as he could on the warm flesh that filled his mouth and glided through his hands. *The sooner I finish him*, he kept repeating to himself, *the sooner this will all be over.* Even so, there was some primitive part of Chris's brain that did not want it to be over so soon. While his conscious mind rationalized and rebelled his body responded with increasing urgency to the taut coils that surrounded his erection. They squeezed enticingly, their ripples and undulations thrilling him in ways he had never imagined. His hips continued their vigorous thrusting even as he struggled to deny the pleasure he was receiving.

Rang let out a long, low groan above him. A quiver in the fingers gripping his head was the only warning Chris received before a throbbing wave started in the base of the monster's erection and raced upward, filling Chris's mouth in an instant with a salty, odd-tasting cream. He gulped it down before he could think and his mouth immediately filled again. Again he swallowed, drinking the monster's pleasure as it poured forth, his hands twitching and clenching around the spasming shaft. His own body tingled and warmth rushed to his face, and as the giant's final spurt rushed over his tongue Chris felt his own loins tensing, his own seed shooting wildly forth. It squished noisily among the coils of tail as it soaked and began to drip from them.

The hand upon Chris's head relaxed its grip entirely, and the clawed fingers began to stroke soothingly at his hair. "Good," Rang's voice purred. "Very good."

Slowly Chris raised his head. A thin trickle of cream glistened upon his chin. He opened his mouth to reply, and then closed it again. Afraid to speak, he peered questioningly into the creature's eyes. Rang smiled back. "Turn around," he rumbled softly.

Numbly Chris obeyed, shuffling around on his knees until he faced away from Rang. He heard scales whispering against one another as Rang squatted behind him. A big, clawed hand settled on his shoulder.

That hand, gentle at first, suddenly shoved him hard. Chris sprawled on his belly with a grunt and before he could roll away he felt the impossible weight of the creature's body descend upon his back. Its thighs pressed down between his own, easily forcing them to the sides and holding them apart. The moist tip of Rang's penis nestled itself ominously between his buttocks.

Chris panicked. "No! Don't do it!" he begged. The creature's penis was nearly as big as his forearm. To even imagine that he could accommodate something that big was ridiculous; Rang, however, seemed eager to try anyway, as though the very real danger of splitting his unwilling lover apart from the inside had never occurred to him.

Or perhaps appealed to him.

Chris screamed in terror and clawed at the floor with his hands. "No! I did what you asked!" he wailed. Rang responded with a cruel chuckle and Chris felt the pressure increase steadily against his anus. "Please, no!" he shrieked but Rang only laughed louder. The pressure became unbearable; Chris felt himself beginning to yield. He fought wildly but could not escape. The creature's immense bulk pinned him down, its chest pressing his face firmly against the floor. He was at the giant's mercy. He felt the massive organ begin to penetrate him, its ungodly girth stretching him painfully wide.

Rang suddenly froze. For several breathless seconds he remained completely motionless, and Chris soon felt the mighty organ shrinking away from his rear. Rang's chest rose up off of his head, and Chris found a magazine being thrust into his face. "Who is this?" Rang bellowed.

Chris blinked in confusion, almost sobbing with relief at having been spared being impaled on Rang's colossal erection. He stared dumbly at the magazine but there was nobody's face on the cover. "Where?" he muttered feebly.

The magazine quivered in front of him and was shoved closer to his nose. The subscription block filled his gaze. "This! Who is this?" The evil hiss had vanished from Rang's voice.

Chris's eyes focused on his own name and address. "That's...that's me," he panted.

The magazine shook harder and then fell to the floor in front of Chris's face. "Oh, no," Rang whimpered. The tone of his voice had changed dramatically. It was as though Chris were hearing a meow coming from the throat of a Rottweiler. "It can't be...it mustn't be..."

Chris managed to catch his breath and tried to move. He was still pinned tightly under the huge creature's body. "What?"

"This address. It's number twenty-one?"

"Y-yes..."

"Oh my..." Rang's hand came down and touched his shoulder hesitantly. "Are you positive it isn't number twenty-seven?"

Chris was utterly bewildered. "It's number twenty-one. I've lived here for years."

"Oh, my God!" Rang suddenly leaped up off of him and staggered backward. Chris heard him bang into the wall, and when he turned his head he saw Rang plastered against the wall with his arms spread out to his sides, all as though Chris had suddenly transformed into something horrific. "This can't be happening. Please, *please* tell me I don't have the wrong address!"

Chris, still shaking, climbed painfully to his feet. He swayed unsteadily and stared at the monster who now seemed more terrified and confused than Chris himself. "What are you talking about?" he wheezed.

Rang fell to his knees and clutched at his head. Tears began to stream from his eyes. "I'm at the wrong address!" he wailed. "I was supposed to go to number twenty-seven. You aren't even a customer!"

"A customer of what?"

"Fantasy Predators, Limited!" Rang bawled from behind his hands. "Number twenty-seven is a subscriber! I can't believe this. I'm going to lose my job!" He suddenly jerked his hands away from his face and gaped at Chris as though he were seeing him for the first time. "You!"

Chris stepped back in alarm.

Rang held out his hands pleadingly. "Oh shit...I...Oh, God, are you hurt? Please tell me you're not hurt!"

Before Chris could respond Rang leaped forward and grabbed him. He dragged Chris's dumbfounded body to the couch and pushed him down onto it and then crouched in front of him. "Take a few deep breaths," Rang said shakily. "Tell me if it hurts anywhere. Can you breathe all right? How many fingers am I holding up?"

"I'm OK," Chris said numbly, and then he frowned, his anger sparking. "But what the hell is this all about? Why did you attack me?"

Rang cowered back as if struck. "I didn't mean to!" he whined. "I mean, I *did* mean to, but I didn't know it was you! That is, I thought you were someone else. You were supposed to be someone else! I got the wrong address – I don't know how! The one looked so much like a seven. Oh, please don't tell my boss! I need this job!"

"All right...*all right*...just be quiet." Chris ran his fingers through his hair and shook his head. "This is crazy. What were you doing, again? You're with...some...fantasy...?"

"Fantasy Predators, Limited. We send professional predators – werewolves, demons, dragons like me – after our subscribers on a pay-per-capture basis. Anything they ask for." Rang looked miserable. "I wouldn't have hurt you, though! We don't hurt our customers. That's the rule. It's only what they ask for. This guy, twenty-seven, contracted for me to..." His voice broke up, and suddenly he threw himself forward, laying his head in Chris's lap and squeezing his eyes shut, tears pouring onto Chris's lap. "Please don't tell them I got the wrong address! They'll fire me! It won't happen again, I swear it, I *swear* it! I'll make it up to you. Anything you ask for! Just name it!

Oh, God, I'm sorry! I can't tell you how sorry I am! I didn't know!" He began to sob hysterically.

Chris could only stare at the blubbering dragon for several long minutes, and then put his hand on the top of Rang's head. "Look... stop crying...stop crying and listen to me."

Sniffling, Rang squeezed a few more tears out of his eyes and opened them. He blinked up at Chris.

"Now, I'm not going to say I'm not mad," Chris continued, "but I can understand how you could have gotten the addresses mixed up. I'm not happy about it, but I'll let it go this time."

Rang lifted his head and wiped at his eyes with a forearm. "You won't tell my boss?" he whispered incredulously.

Chris shook his head. "I won't tell him this time. I just want you to leave and we'll forget this happened."

Rang's face lit up and his fiery eyes swirled with relief. "Oh, thank you!" He snatched Chris up in a hug that almost crushed the man, and then just as quickly let him go. "Oh, sorry! I'm sorry!" He brushed off Chris's shoulders. "Are you sure you're OK? I really need to know that you're OK."

"I'm fine. Just get out."

"I'll pay for your clothes. Send the bill. I'll pay for them. I promise."

"Whatever. Just leave."

"You're so nice! Thank you for being so understanding. I really don't know how this could have happened. When I saw the seven I really thought..."

"Just *go!*"

"Right, right!" Rang scrambled to his feet and scurried to the door. "If there's anything I can do to make it up to you, I want you to name it, anything at all. I owe you big time."

"GO!!"

Rang yelped and dove through the door, yanking it shut behind him with a bang.

Still in shock, Chris wobbled to the window and peered outside. He watched as Rang ran up the street and stopped at number twenty-seven. The dragon squinted closely at the house number, and then stood back and looked at the numbers on both sides. Hastily he composed himself and knocked on the door, and a few seconds later he burst into the house. "I am Rang!" his voice thundered distantly, "And you are mine!"

Chris kept watching until the door to number twenty-seven was slammed violently shut, and then made his way back to the sofa and collapsed. He lay in silence, staring into space. Now and then his gaze would wander to the shredded remains of his clothing scattered across the foyer, then up to the gouges carved by Rang's horns in the ceiling.

The sun was setting. Chris's whole body felt numb, save for his aching jaw and rear. He became aware of something upon his chin and traced the line of the dragon-semen, now dry. Slowly he reached for the telephone and dialed. "I want the number for Fantasy Predators, Limited," he mumbled.

A moment later a cheerful voice sang, "Good afternoon, Fantasy Predators, making your darkest dreams come true, all major credit cards accepted, how may I help you?"

Chris rubbed at his shoulder where four thin lines were darkening to red. He said nothing for a moment.

"Hello?"

"Oh...yes. Um...can I ask...do you have a dragon on your payroll... named Rang?"

"Just a moment." Scratchy music played as he was put on hold, and then, "Yes, we do, Sir. Sorry for the wait – had to look him up. He's new."

Chris staring at the ruins of his shirt by the door. He could still hear the sound the great talons had made as they sliced through the fabric.

"Hello?"

"Uh...yes, I'm still here."

"Yes sir, is there something I can help you with?"

Chris ran his finger along his chin once more, tracing the thin line up to his lip. "Yes," he said, and then cleared his throat. "Yes, there is. I'd like to place an order, please..."

Havoc

"United Six-Five-Six, traffic left, declaring an emergency!"

Those were the last words that were received as horrified controllers watched a second signal appear beside that of the big jet. A moment later the two merged, and to the astonishment of everyone watching they slowed to a halt and hovered impossibly in place.

It was nearly at that same moment that Havoc was circling his prospective mate. The dragon had been without a suitable female for centuries and desire was burning as hot as his fiery breath within him as he drew alongside his choice. She was perfect, big, like him, sleek and beautiful – and interested, as she demonstrated by rolling once, exposing her underside to him before coyly lifting a wing and banking away. The air began to whistle around Havoc's thick malehood as it emerged from the slit in his underbelly. He was ready. Anxious to begin, he dove after her.

It is a fact that male dragons become so overwhelmed by the euphoria of mating that they sink into something of a trance and become unaware of their surroundings, their concentration fixed solely on catching the female in flight, but this time the experience was far more intense than anything Havoc had ever before experienced. His vision blurred and he felt as though he were falling, no longer in control of his own flight. But his wings were still pumping steadily, and after a moment he felt the wind rushing across them once more. *Too long*, he thought. *It has been far too long.*

The air was suddenly cooler, the sky brighter, but Havoc took no notice. His eyes saw nothing; he could sense only the presence of the female as he drew up above her. With a guttural roar he dropped and threw his forelegs around the female's body, pulling her against his belly, thrusting himself deep into her.

Passengers in the rearmost seats of Flight 656 never felt a thing when the tail section of the jumbo jet was suddenly wrenched up and off. Suction tore through the cabin as it decompressed; startlingly, though, the rush of air ceased abruptly. Only a few of the passengers had time to turn and see a massive, bright-red dome plugging the hole before it surged forward, tearing seats free and flinging shrieking bodies ahead of it. It crashed through the length of the rear cabin, smearing some hapless souls against the walls as it passed, crushing others tightly against the bulkhead. For a moment it rested there, pulsating, a large crevice at its tip yawning and dripping clear fluid.

For a brief moment a stunned silence hung over the cabin, but the screams began anew as the red dome withdrew and then slammed forward again, collapsing the bulkhead and bursting into the center cabin. The fuselage crumpled behind it as it began to plunge like a piston, each stroke driving it further and further into the aircraft, piling up more and more bodies ahead of it as the frantic passengers clawed their way forward.

Soon there was nowhere to go. The pounding dome battered repeatedly at the tangle of humanity, compressing them into a tighter and tighter mass. Very few were left alive to witness the crevice at the tip of the dome quiver and gape open, gushing hundreds gallons of a thick, white fluid which filled the First Class section. The flood burned like acid, searing everything that it touched, and the suffering of the helpless survivors was mercifully cut short as the aircraft finally came apart.

Havoc moaned as his pleasure poured forth and he relaxed, his only movements the beating of his wings to hold him aloft. It had been beautiful, simply beautiful, more beautiful than he could have ever dreamed. This would be the first of many, he knew. Dragons often mated dozens of times during the brief season, driven by a feral lust that once kindled could barely be controlled. And he had been without for so, so long. Gradually he began to grow more aware of his surroundings. His vision cleared at last.

WHAT?

His roar of surprise quickly turned into an ominous growl. Furious, he tore the bizarre shining object to pieces between his claws. What was the meaning of this? Where was his mate? And what in the world was this flimsy metal shell doing up here?

Havoc hurled the wreckage aside and peered about. Only now did he begin to realize that things had changed dramatically. Everything seemed strange to him. The sun was an odd color. The magnetic fields he sensed were all wrong. What was happening? Where was he? This could not be real. Not after he had waited for so long. Not when he had finally found his ideal mate!

Arching his back, Havoc dove down through the clouds to try to find his bearings. The landscape he saw below him when he broke into the clear had changed as well. It was grey and rocky, rather dismal, and quite definitely not the same land he had just left. Burning with disappointment and the unquenched mating-urge, he backwinged and dropping to the ground, where he landed in the midst of a maze of stone towers and canyons. It stank here, worse than his own breath did after an accidental backflash. It was a stale, smoky smell, mixed with decay. The unpleasant surroundings only fueled the flames of his rage.

He took one step forward. Something crackled wetly under his foot, and glancing downward he noticed for the first time the buzzing activity all around him. Tiny figures milled about, shying away from the foot that had landed in their midst. They swarmed in a confused mass all along the floor of the maze as far as he could see. Annoyed at their high-pitching squealing he lashed out with a kick, sending dozens of them tumbling through the air.

Something about them struck him as familiar and he bent to scoop a few of them up in his fingers for a closer inspection. A disdainful sneer crossed his muzzle. Humans! So it was these crawling little vermin who were responsible for this outrage. They had given him more than their share of trouble in the past, but this time they had gone too far. How dare they steal him away from his mate when he had been on the verge of claiming her at last? How dare they mock him with the indignity of that flying metal contraption!

With a scowl he closed his fist, squashing the insolent little pests into a sticky mass which he grumblingly shook from his fingers. So, the humans presumed to toy with a dragon in his mating season, did they? Very well, then. So be it. He would play their little game.

And he was going to enjoy it.

The floor of the rock canyon was carpeted with thousands of fat, squirming little bodies that crunched noisily as he trampled on them. He paid them no heed, preoccupied for now on finding something to quench the fire in his loins. His eyes soon fell upon a likely target: a long, metallic serpent crawling along the ground. It seemed about the right size, and if it was at all like the metal plaything he'd found in the sky, it should provide him at least a momentary distraction. He would see to the humans afterward.

Stalking toward the serpent, he stooped and grasped it firmly behind its head, which much to his surprise simply came loose. The entire beast, he discovered, was assembled in pieces, and as he lifted this first segment to his face he could just barely see countless tiny eyes staring back at him from within its transparent flanks.

Havoc let out a mirthful roar. "Well!" he bellowed, placing his eye right against the thin metal shell to gaze at the panic-stricken humans packed within. "This is most interesting indeed. Well, little ones, Havoc has come, as you desired." He tossed that first segment aside, and placed a foot on either side of the remainder which lay motionless beneath him. "And as it seems to have been your summons that removed me from my mate's back, I think it only fair that you perform in her stead."

His member had already emerged and in Havoc's fevered state it needed very little urging to reach its full size. Slowly he lowered himself to all fours, and then with a sneer he squatted lower. The second car of the train was pressed flat as the dragon's haunches settled upon it, the passengers within shrieking in short-lived agony. Scales as hard as steel grated on the roof of the third car, pinning it in place as the dragon's mammoth penis pressed relentlessly against and finally burst through the leading end. Havoc rumbled in delight at the feeling of countless little bodies wriggling against his most sensitive flesh. He had not expected such a pleasure. "Ahhh, yes, that is nice!" he hissed, and digging his talons into the ground he began to thrust, slowly and powerfully, his organ driving itself again and again into the screaming mass. He was half aware of other little forms darting around his hands and feet; for now, though, he ignored them. "Don't run, humans," he snorted. "Don't tire yourselves. Every one of you will serve as mates for me before I am through." He thrust harder, beginning to pant, his tongue curling up over the top of his muzzle. The caress of so many limbs and torsos and faces against him drove his passion to new heights. After only a few breathless moments he uttered a roar that shattered glass great distances away. His seed spewed violently into the coach, wave after wave, until it rolled from the empty windowpanes in a surreal and ponderous tide.

Havoc drew a deep breath and heaved himself upward, rising to his feet with the crumpled train car, dripping semen and gore, still impaled on his erection. He laughed when he saw a few hapless survivors writhing at his feet. Coated in his cream, they shrieked and flailed as the flesh was eaten rapidly from their bones. "Poor humans," he jeered. "Is the dragon's seed not to your liking?" He stayed and watched them until they stopped moving, and then with a jerk of his hips he sent the coach hurtling into the side of a nearby building.

In spite of his release the ache, he realized bitterly, had not subsided. Deep down in his loins it gnawed at him still, the humans in their metal snake having done little to appease him. They were simply not enough, not at all a substitute for a proper mate, and this made Havoc ever more resentful. Growling, he stooped and snatched up the surviving train cars, twisted them to wreckage in his hands and tossed them away. Then he turned his attention to those who had escaped his initial assault and were now fleeing with countless others through the rock canyon. In their panic they were not even trying to hide. "Mindless insects," he spat as he watched them streaming around the massive footprints he had left. With only three long steps he was upon them.

The humans squealed and veered away from his foot as it crashed down to the ground. He took another step, chuckling scornfully as the entire pack veered again to the other side. Havoc began to march forward very slowly, herding them back and forth with every footfall. "Oh no! Oh no! Look out!" he said mockingly. "The big dragon is going to step on you!" His taunting stoked them into a frenzied flight which only added to his sport. He lifted one foot over them, allowing it to hover only long enough for the nimblest of them to escape from its ominous shadow before he let it fall. For a moment he simply rested there, feeling the little sluggards writhing beneath it, and then shifted his weight onto it, feeling them pop one by one before the ground finally gave way. Killing them was cruelly satisfying and he did so repeatedly, step after step, thinning their ranks while jeering and tormenting them until only one was left alive. That one darted out from underfoot twice more before Havoc managed to trap it under one huge toe. Rather than crushing it, though, he lifted that foot away and strode onward, leaving the shivering man bruised but still breathing in his wake.

"Your agility has earned you your life, for now," he snarled over his shoulder. "Run, now. Tell your worthless lot that Havoc Emberwing has come to teach them what it means to trifle with a dragon." He moved on, striding purposefully along the now-deserted street, searching for further sport and further relief.

Far from the scene of the dragon's rampage a singular man was fighting through streets packed with fleeing citizenry, but unlike them he was clawing his way closer to the carnage. Professor Norden paid almost as little attention to the mob around him as the dragon himself did; wracked with guilt, he could think of nothing other than how he might stop the massacre that he had unleashed.

My fault. The words seared into his thoughts – my fault – like a hot branding iron. *My fault.* Unceasing, unbearable, until he yearned to take his own life just to silence them. Indeed, he had nearly done just that mere seconds before he heard the monster speak for the first time. The newscast had been brief but it had been long enough to let Norden hear the godlike voice bellowing out taunts and challenges until a shadow had fallen over the reporter and the picture had gone to static. The dragon had spoken. If it could speak, Norden desperately hoped, then surely it could be reasoned with. How, though, to make such a monster listen to him?

It will listen, he told himself. It has to listen, because I am the only one on Earth who can send it back to where it came from.

Ahead of him he could hear the crash of buildings being torn apart and thousands of screaming voices that were all but drowned out by the angry giant's roars. *My fault.* For the hundredth time Norden stumbled, nearly crushed beneath the weight of those words alone. He had to move faster; every second meant hundreds of lives lost, perhaps thousands. He prayed that the dragon would pass closely enough for him to catch its notice, and moreover that it would spare him long enough to hear his offer.

It did not take long for Havoc to catch up to the fleeing populace. He found them swarming through a wide corridor that ended in a cul-de-sac from which only two narrow channels afforded escape. The resulting bottleneck trapped thousands of them in a seething, screaming mass. He shook his head, astonished at the depths of their stupidity, and for a moment he felt sorry for them.

It was a very brief moment, however. Dull though they were, these little pests were responsible for his missing a very crucial opportunity and Havoc was not about to allow that to go unpunished. He stamped slowly and deliberately into their midst, amusing himself for a while simply by crushing them underfoot. The scent of blood reached his nostrils as the number of dead rose; it created another stirring, this time in his belly, and Havoc was suddenly reminded of how long it had been since he had enjoyed a proper meal. No matter. Humans had satisfied his hunger many times in the past, and at that moment there were more than enough of them.

Havoc crouched and then dropped to all fours. With his jaws gaping wide he lowered his head and thrust it forward into the crowd, shoveling scores of writhing bodies into his mouth. He swallowed them whole, as is a dragon's habit with small prey, and took a moment to enjoy their frantic little struggles as they slid, still alive, into his stomach before capturing another mouthful. With such a vast number trapped before him he was able to eat at a leisurely pace, a rare luxury for him. Soon his belly was full and contented, and even then it appeared as though he had barely thinned the herd. It seemed a terrible waste to be full so soon when so many of them were still alive.

He would have to remedy that.

Rising to his feet again, Havoc took a moment to lick away the remains of those who had fallen beneath his hands, and then he arched his neck downward, his mouth open. The air before him began to ripple with waves of heat that soon exploded into a colossal fireball. Flames roared downward and flowed along the street like a river, silencing the screams of the crowd in a matter of seconds and leaving behind a sea of charred, crackling flesh.

Havoc smiled as he surveyed his handiwork. Cooked meat had such a pleasant aroma. It occurred to him that in all his long life he had never bothered to taste it so he stooped to pick out a sample, and as he did so he felt raindrops pattering upon his back.

No, it was not raindrops. Curious, Havoc stood and turned around, and a few more struck on his arm. It was fire, a rain of fire. He stared, momentarily confused, as more and more little orange puffs burst against him, barely smudging his scales, and then he chuckled thunderously. "Well, well," he said with a grin. "At last they have decided to fight back." He squinted and searched the streets and rooftops below but could not locate this new adversary, and then he felt a burst upon the crown of his head. Gazing upward he spied a flock of tiny silver insects buzzing in the sky overhead. They looked like miniature replicas of the mockup dragon that the humans had first used to taunt him. Puffs of smoke rose from under their wings seconds before the fireballs popped against his hide.

Havoc was intrigued. "How clever," he said aloud. "They mimic the dragon." He noticed that they were flying lower with each pass, emboldened no doubt by his lack of response. *Maybe not so clever after all*, he thought. Rearing up to his full height he raked his hand through the swarm, missing them at first but with a second wipe he managed to snatch one from the air. Its wings crumpled in his fingers, laughably fragile, and as he brought it to his face for a closer examination he saw a tiny human perched on its back. "So that's it!" He poked curiously at the flier and was startled when flame sputtered from its back and its human rider was thrown, saddle and all, into the air. As Havoc watched, a plume of white silk rose from the saddle, leaving the rider drifting like a seed on the wind.

Laughing, Havoc caught the plume between two fingers, lifting it up high so that the shrieking rider dangled before his nose. "A feeble, yet noble effort, Little One," he rumbled, "and for that I shall kill you quickly." His long tongue flicked out and curled behind the little man, dragging it into his mouth and thrusting it between his teeth. His jaws closed firmly, and the silken plume fluttered limply to the ground.

The other fliers had darted off and were circling out of his reach. *At least they were not completely stupid*, he thought. Still, he was not about to tolerate such insolence. Massive wings snapped out and swept downward as the dragon leaped into the air, the shock wave pulverizing buildings and people in a huge radius from where he had been standing. He beat his wings hard, climbing rapidly to where the fliers were beginning to scatter. Smirking, he swatted at them with both hands, batting several from the sky and sending them hurtling to earth in flames. He caught one with a quick grab and broke off one of its wings to find out how well it could fly that way: not well, apparently. Another one burst apart as his tail snapped against it. A few more were sent whirling out of control after being caught in the blast of his wings. Some of the riders managed to leap off of their mounts and floated off on their silks; Havoc was amused when one of the shrouds caught fast on his right horn and he decided to let it stay just to see how long its owner would last.

Soon only a single flier was left in the air and Havoc set off after it. This one was feisty. It darted left as he fell in behind it, then rolled and spun in the opposite direction. Havoc followed close behind, matching its erratic course, slowly closing the gap. It broke right; he mirrored it, his head maintaining a fixed position in the flier's wake. The rider grew more frantic, his maneuvers more desperate, but the dragon had a lifetime of experience in pursuing prey like this. Havoc's body curled and looped through the air while his gaping jaws slowly inched forward until the flier was between them.

Havoc arched and dove downward as his teeth crunched down on the flimsy flier. An acrid taste spewed from it when he squashed it against the roof of his mouth with his tongue, and he spat the wreckage out with a snort as he backwinged and landed. He suddenly remembered the one he'd snagged in flight, and reached up to tug the silk from his horn. To his disappointment the rider had not survived, its frail body torn apart by his violent flight. He twisted it loose from the silk and tossed the body aside. The silk itself fluttered downward, coming to rest draped across his massive penis, erect from the excitement of the chase. The airy caress reminded Havoc of his still-unsatisfied mating urge. The burning in his loins still demanded to be quenched, and the touch of the silk had given the dragon an idea.

He strode purposefully through the city, shouldering aside the fragile buildings until he found a suitably wide valley swarming with fleeing humans. He plodded toward them slowly, driving them ahead of him with his feet. Those who were too slow were simply squashed to death; the rest stampeded before him like cattle before the lightning, their numbers building up quickly, the mob's growing density slowing their flight until they were barely moving. Havoc stood behind them, snickering at how easily they could be herded, and then reached for them. He was unaware of the tiny, singular figure staggering up behind him.

Professor Norden gasped as he stumbled through the street, clutching the megaphone tightly to his chest to keep it from being knocked away. The tall buildings blocked his view; he had no idea where the dragon was, and the sounds of destruction and carnage seemed to come from all directions. He had to fight harder and harder against the rush of people fleeing in the opposite direction, so he knew that he had to be getting close.

He came upon a major intersection where hundreds of people were rushing to the left. The dragon, he reasoned, must be approaching from the other direction. Norden pressed onward, struggling to stay close to the buildings but the stampeding humanity knocked him into the street. He heard tires squealing, and looked up in time to see the grille of a taxi cab bearing down on him.

No, he thought, *not this! I can't die like this! I have to send that monster back!* Norden tried to move his feet but they would not obey. He was frozen like a deer on the highway. The taxi bore down upon him, the driver's face wild and frantic. The hood and fenders were dented and smeared with blood. It was obvious he had no intention of swerving or even slowing down in his desperation to escape.

A shadow fell. Metal crashed. In one instant Norden was staring at a taxi rushing toward him, and in the next he was staring at a set of enormous, curved talons. Shaking, unsure if he was alive or not, Norden slowly raised his head. His gaze traveled up along a powerful leg to a long, muscular tail weaving side to side. His heart pounded in his chest, and finally he was able to muster enough control over his legs to stumble to one side. The dragon's gigantic toes curled as its foot lifted skyward, talons kicking back the flattened wreckage of the cab. Norden gaped, awestruck, as the mighty foot glided through the air, the muscles of the leg flexing elegantly while the toes spread once again and descended.

Norton's awe turned to horror as that foot came down heavily upon those who had fled past him just seconds before. He saw them stumble, knocked down by the scaly sole as it covered them, and then he saw arms and legs twitching from under it for a split second before the heel sank into the pavement. And then when it lifted again....

Professor Norden choked and somehow managed to keep his breakfast in. With a despairing groan he staggered after the rampaging beast. There was no way that he could catch its attention from behind, and it was clear that he would never catch up to it now. In only a few paces it had already outdistanced him. He had to find some way of getting on front of it again.

His prayers were answered when the dragon suddenly stopped. Norden broke into a run, crying out in horror as from behind he watched the beast crouch and begin groping among the panicked crowd that had been driven ahead of it. In desperation Norden darted into the lobby of a nearby hotel. The elevator doors were open but the power was off, so Professor Norden started the long, breathless climb up the stairs to the roof.

Havoc smiled as he squatted, scanning the sea of terrified faces below him. His penis throbbed insistently; he so looked forward to the pleasure that these little gnats were once more going to provide for him. "Stop squealing," he grunted scornfully as he cleared a spot ahead of him with a sweep of his hand and stretched the silk out on the ground. "It is as I said: you brought this upon yourselves when you stole me from my mate, and so it is you who must now serve as mates for me." He lowered both hands and began to scoop the squirming bodies onto it. "I would think you would feel honored." He gathered up the edges of the silk, using his fingers to poke any stragglers back inside as he fashioned it into a sack, and then with a low growl he shoved his penis down hard into the open end.

Instant pleasure rushed through him as his member sank into the wriggling mass. He held the edges of the makeshift bag closed around the base of his erection with one hand, and with the other began to squeeze at the bulging end, the writhing against his flesh becoming wilder still. "Ah, yes," he crooned, and squeezed them harder. His hips twitched, thrusting the thick organ into the tightening mass, his senses growing dim with the rising passion.

It was all over far too soon and with a roar he poured his seed into his captives' midst. Flesh hissed as it melted away and the desperate thrashing within the bag quickly faded to nothing. Havoc sighed and let the bag fall to the ground, revealing nothing but bones left within.

Pleasing, he thought, yet still not entirely satisfying. He pondered what he might do next to punish these little gnats, but then he heard a voice behind him. It was a proper voice, not the grating little squeak that humans make. Turning, Havoc was startled to see nobody there – only a single paltry human standing atop a nearby stone block. Sneering, Havoc raised an immense hand to smash it to bits.

"Dragon!"

Havoc's hand stopped in mid-descent and he narrowed his eyes. The voice had definitely come from that one human. Frowning, he lowered his head and peered suspiciously at the diminutive creature. "Who addresses me?" he said icily.

"I do!" Professor Norden shouted into the megaphone. "You mustn't continue killing those people. I am the one who brought you here."

Havoc's eyes widened and a grin broke across his muzzle. "Ah, I see. So the wizard finally reveals himself." He snaked his head down closer, almost touching the little man with his nose. "And what gives you the right to tell Havoc Emberwing what he must and must not do?"

"Because I am the only one who can send you back. And I will do so, if you will only allow me time to make adjustments to my instruments."

"If? *IF?*" Havoc threw his head back and roared with laughter. "There is no *if*, Puny One! You will send me back, or you will watch every last one of your kind die beneath my feet."

Professor Norden's ears rang from the booming of the dragon's voice. "But I must adjust the instruments first! If you will only stop killing my people, stop destroying our city, I swear that I will work as quickly as I can, and will have you home before the end of the day."

Havoc's tongue slowly slid from his lips and passed thoughtfully across the top of his muzzle as he considered the offer. At last he shook his head. "I've a better idea," he said, lowering his eye close to the little wizard. "I think that I am going to continue killing, and I am going to continue destroying your pathetic little city. Only when you are prepared to return me to my home will I stop. That should give you ample incentive to work quickly."

"No!"

Havoc bared his teeth. "Insolent gnat!" he bellowed and landed a murderous stomp upon the people cowering at his feet. "After the anguish you have caused me, I think that I am being extremely magnanimous to leave any of your worthless kind alive. Now be off. Get to your work. I shall continue to entertain myself until you are through." With that he turned his back, eyeing the people below and lifting his foot.

"Wait!" Norden pleaded.

Havoc tensed then spun about, tail smashing through an apartment building across the street. "You filthy...you *dare* to command me...!"

"Please! Please forgive me! It's just that it will take time for me to get to my laboratory. I can begin working immediately if you take me there."

Havoc glowered and clenched his teeth. "I am no steed, Wizard," he spat. "But if it will return me to my mate more quickly, then I will deign to carry you." With that he reached a blood-smeared hand down and caught Professor Norden between two fingers, then deposited the trembling human into the palm of his hand. "Where is this laboratory?"

Professor Norden cowered for a moment in the dragon's hand, overwhelmed, until Havoc's teeth showed angrily and he scrambled to his feet. "It's...there," he said, pointing into the distance. "That building with the spire. Do you see?"

"I see." The dragon strode forward, leaving the survivors of his rampage behind. Norden's relief did not last, however, as Havoc chose not to make his way through the streets but rather to march in a devastating straight line. Professor Norden closed his eyes tightly and tried to shut out the sound of buildings being smashed, of helpless people being crushed to death under the dragon's feet as he plowed toward the Institute. He could not stop the destruction, but he could still try to save as many lives as he could by ridding the world of the dragon. It could never atone for the sin of having brought Havoc to Earth in the first place, but at least the carnage would end at last.

Havoc kicked irritably through a hotel and stepped into the courtyard of the Institute building. There he lowered his hand, allowing Professor Norden to slide off onto the roof. "Now get to work," he growled. "You will give me a sign when you are through." Before Professor Norden could say anything, Havoc had turned again and thundered away.

The laboratory was deserted but thankfully still had power. Professor Norden tore open the front of the console and began the task of rewiring. He tried to concentrate on the task at hand without letting the crushing remorse cloud his thinking. It was nearly impossible, however. The creature was here because of him, because of a forbidden experiment that he had chosen to undertake regardless. None of his colleagues, not even his students were to know of his research. The knowledge, and the glory, were to be his and his alone.

And now the responsibility for the deaths of thousands of innocent people was his alone, and every second that he spent meant a dozen more. He completed the rewiring through a blur of tears.

After struggling to the roof with the remote console he fumbled with the tangle of power cables. He could see the dragon's towering form in the distance, stooping and rising to stuff something into its jaws. Choking back a sob, Professor Norden connected the final wire to the rooftop spire, his makeshift antenna, and then ran to the edge of the roof to...

...to what? With a groan Professor Norden realized that he had neglected to ask the dragon just *how* he might be signaled. The megaphone was useless; Havoc was too far off. With every second that passed more people were dying. Frantic, Norden, dashed downstairs to fetch a bottle of magnesium from the laboratory. Scrambling back to the rooftop he dumped the entire contents of the bottle and struck a match. The resulting blaze of light nearly blinded him. He staggered back, covering his eyes, unable to see but able to feel the crash of approaching footfalls.

The magnesium burned itself out. Slowly Professor Norden uncovered his eyes. Ahead of him loomed the armored scales of the dragon's chest, and above them — Norden stifled a cry at the sight of the monster's jaws crammed with living people, their limbs waving frantically from between the cage of its teeth. He could only watch helplessly as the dragon threw its head back. Its throat bulged, and when it lowered its head again its mouth was empty. Professor Norden could still hear countless muffled screams.

Havoc licked his lips. "You are finished?"

Professor Norden fumbled for the megaphone, sickened by the horrible demonstration. "Yes," he stammered. "I'm ready."

"Good." The dragon glared down. "Proceed."

Professor Norden shivered and set the megaphone down. He glanced over the remote console for a few seconds and prayed that he had made the connections properly. Holding his breath, he keyed in the sequence, and then pressed the button that he had labeled "commit." In the lab below the converters begin to drone, steadily powering up. The sound grew louder, its pitch rising; the spire-antenna began to hum and glowed slightly, and Professor Norden prayed as he had never prayed before.

The sound that split the air when the machine's whine reached its peak was like a hundred lightning bolts crackling at once. Havoc closed his eyes as shadows swirled through his head. It was the same experience as before, the brief, faded consciousness, the roaring silence, the sensation of falling. Only when the feeling had passed and the crackling died away did he open his eyes again. He turned his head slowly, gazing around at the smashed ruins of the city, at the billows of smoke, and then at the bewildered little human standing next to the smoking remains of his instrument. He scowled. "Do not dare toy with me, Wizard, or..."

An angry roar from the sky interrupted his threat. Above him circled the female, as confused and outraged as he had himself been upon his arrival. She caught sight of him below and swooped, passing low overhead and then rising up high in a graceful climb. She roared again and then trilled questioningly.

Havoc slowly lowered his gaze back down to the wide-eyed wizard on the rooftop and drew his lips back into a dangerous smile. Before Professor Norden could move the dragon had caught him. "Thank you," Havoc said simply. He lifted the little man up to the top of the spire, put a finger on his back, and pressed Norden's belly down firmly on the spire until he felt the point poke through to his fingertip. "Your services are no longer required." With that he turned away and crouched, his tail crashing into the front half of the building and crumpling it. The dust cloud had hardly settled when he was once again airborne, his powerful wings stirring a hurricane as he rose toward the waiting female.

The female hissed as he approached, still unnerved by the sudden change of scenery. Havoc crooned soothingly as he approached her; as she relaxed, he twined his neck around hers and nuzzled at her ear. "Don't fret, my dear one," he whispered, "I suspect that we are going to be very happy here."

Jailbird

Tiren swore under his breath as another bolt struck just aft of the main thruster. Maybe "you'll never take me alive" had been the wrong thing to say. "Come on, Baby," he pleaded as more of his console turned to red and warning klaxons blared through the compartment. "Come on, Sweetheart, hold together for Daddy." Another hit sent the ship into a wild spin. The strobes on the police cruisers streaked like meteors past his viewports until he managed to stabilize his flight, just in time to dodge another bolt.

Gateway Nineteen hove into view and Tiren made for it with as much speed as he could squeeze out of his damaged power cells. The cops would not dare to shoot in the direction of the Gateway unless they wanted to try outrunning a supernova. All he had to do was stay ahead of them for another few seconds. He urged his ship onward. Only a few more seconds and he would be out of planetary jurisdiction, and free. He had no idea what awaited him in the Void but he did not care. Where ever he turned up did not matter as long as there was no more prison food, no more electroharness, nobody waiting to shank him around every corner. "So long, suckers," he sneered as the Gateway powered up ahead of him. "Ti is home free!"

Or so it seemed. Frenetically dancing lights filled his forward viewport as a cruiser darted between Tiren's ship and the Gateway. Startled, Tiren hit the thrusters but even before his ship's course began to deflect his mind filled with images of the leering cops as they bound him and rammed him over and over from behind before flinging him down into the Hole yet again. "No way," he growled and re-corrected his course for the Gateway. "This time, this one is going to fuck you right back." As the cruiser's strobes centered themselves in his viewport he jammed his claw down so hard on the thruster that it pierced the control switch.

The cruiser was twice the size of his ship and growing larger with each passing second. Tiren's beak was clamped so tightly that his whole neck ached but he kept the strobe above the cruiser's cabin dead in the middle of his viewport. "Your turn to take it up the ass now, Boys," he hissed. The cruiser loomed, filling the viewport now, bigger and bigger until that single strobe, throbbing like a pulsar, was all that Tiren could see. The collision alert wailed.

The pulsar dropped abruptly downward and out of sight, followed by the letters L-I-C and then a welcome view of the Gateway's yawning throat, but then there was a jarring impact that sent the Gateway spinning around his viewport. Sirens howled in a raucous symphony around him. The sound was quickly muffled into silence beneath an overwhelming sensation of being stretched into a thin, thin wire. A wave of nausea sent the contents of his crop bursting from his beak. "Gah...I should have cast that up before I left," he croaked.

The disorientation and the nausea passed and Tiren angrily silenced the alarms. Details of the damage scrolled frantically along the computer readout. Both fuel and air were bleeding out. The computer, ever helpful, was recommending a return to his point of origin. "No fucking way," he said aloud. The pellet that he had cast floated past his eyes, almost as though it were taunting him. It was nothing but paper and bits of fiber – typical prison fare. "No way am I ever coughing one of those up again." Instead he entered the destination *planet, unspecified*. The computer asked for his requirements. *No UPD jurisdiction, air, water...*

"In that order," he muttered. He would have liked more options but a previously quiet horn started to howl. The readout screen turned red. Power levels critical. Oxygen levels critical. Emergency beacon activating. Override? *Yes*. Are you sure? *Yes*.

He braced himself against another round of nausea and the feeling that his legs were being forced up into his skull. Stars appeared in his viewports, and dead ahead lay a gorgeous and shiny planet. *UPD jurisdiction?* he queried. None, the computer replied, and then the readout went blank.

"Uh-oh," Tiren whispered. Every indicator in the cabin fell dark. The air circulators stopped hissing. "Oh, this is so not good," he said. The only light now was that which bounced off of the planet's surface, something he could not help noticing was approaching very rapidly. There had not been enough power to slow his approach, let alone prepare for re-entry. He jabbed at the thruster switch: nothing. The planet grew rapidly until the viewport showed nothing but a wall of blue. The ship started to shudder, then to shake violently as brilliant yellow flames burst across the viewport.

Tiren raked the cover off of the hatch release and grasped the handle. It occurred to him suddenly that this might not be the actual plant that the computer had selected for re-entry. What if he was supposed to have maneuvered around this one to the next world in line before the ship's computer ran out of juice? He might pop the hatch and end up sucking ammonia. That notion was not a pleasant one, but all told it seemed better than roasting to a cinder in the rapidly-disintegrating ship. "Here goes nothing," he mumbled, twisted the handle, and yanked hard.

The blast knocked him senseless. He was dimly aware of tumbling end over end, of raw wind tearing at his feathers until finally his instincts took over and he snapped both wings open wide. They caught the wind and held, a little singed at the edges but apparently none the worse for wear. The horizon stopped spinning. Fresh, cool air without even a hint of ammonia flooded into his lungs. Below him was a sea of blue, which, when he focused the telefield of his eye upon it, he realized was a vast expanse of water. It stretched clear to the horizon both left and right, and as far forward as he could see and as far back.

Air. Water. And nothing else, damn it. "Fucking computer!" he growled. The machines were so damned literal. If it had dropped him on some desolate water world he was going to...well, there was not much worse he could do. The remains of his ship were coming apart below him, the computer separating itself into a million streams of glowing, liquefied metal behind which a black plume trailed in a forlorn spiral. There was no question that Tiren was going to be staying for the long haul.

Angrily he smacked down a fleeting spark of panic. There were rising thermal columns all around, enough to keep him aloft for days if need be. He flapped for the nearest one and dove into its base to start a lazy circle upward. At the apex he drifted off and rode the planet's prevailing winds toward the sun in a long glide that carried him to another thermal. He sailed that way for hours over endless blue water, until just when that annoying spark was starting to rekindle he caught a glimpse of land at the far reach of his telefield. "Fuck, yeah!" he crowed.

He knew that he was not off the hook yet. That quick glance had been enough to show a landscape with lines that were far too straight and regular to be natural formations. Just like any planet with any appreciable oxygen levels, this one was probably inhabited, and even if the UPD had no claim on him here there was no telling if the locals had established an extradition treaty, and even if not, he could not assume that they were the sort who looked kindly on strangers. He circled higher, until the air grew thin and frigid and his lungs burned. It turned out to be a wise decision; when he reached the shoreline he could see the unmistakable outlines of cities below. His telefield showed him dense clusters of buildings with barely-distinct forms moving amongst them. They made him curious but he was not about to drop down for a closer look. If he could not see them, chances were good that they could not see him, and that suited Tiren just fine.

He let the winds carry him further inland to where the structures were less dense and open spaces began to appear between them. Perfect. Banking, Tiren glided from his thermal and splayed his wings wide, angling them to let the air slip past and drop him into a steady, controlled descent. He aimed for a hilly region between two of the structures where the vegetation was dense and would offer him cover. It was none too soon, too, since he had not eaten since the breakout and his crop felt like it was going to gnaw itself apart. If the yokels below were friendly maybe he could beg a scrap or two out of them. If not, well, he had plenty of other ways to get what he wanted.

"What the hell??"

A shadow on the ground below was approaching fast. Tiren jerked his head around to see what was coming at him but the sky was empty. The horizon was high – way too high. He looked down again and realized just in time to brace himself that the streaking shadow was his own.

His feet hit hard and his legs buckled, sending him crashing to the ground where the breath was knocked clean out of him. For a moment he simply lay gasping, his mind awhirl, trying to figure out how he could have so badly misjudged his landing. He looked around for cover but found none, only a bed of low and scrubby bushes. Maybe he had blacked out and been blown off course. The planet could have had some toxin in the atmosphere that screwed with his senses.

With a grunt Tiren climbed to his feet. He flexed – wings first, then arms, then legs, then back. A few bruises, a broken feather here and there, but nothing that would ground him and no broken bones. He examined the vegetation beneath him and concluded that it was indeed the same terrain that he had seen from the sky. The plants, though, were barely as high as his knees. What he had assumed to be nearby structures must have been something else that had made the foliage appear much larger, which then created the illusion that the ground was much further away. It was an honest mistake. Could have happened to anyone.

But wait. Those *were* structures.

Tiren squinted. They were much closer than he had thought them to be, only a few steps away, but they were definitely buildings, and it was soon clear that they were dwellings because something came scurrying out when he cautiously approached. Some sort of bug, it seemed. Two of them – wingless, upright, squeaky. Curious, he trapped one beneath his foot and stooped to snag the other between his fingers, bringing it to his face for a close look. It was not a bug at all, he realized, since it had no shell and he could feel tiny bones breaking inside when he squeezed it. Rolling it into his palm he sliced it open with a claw and pulled out its innards. It squealed and bled red, a sight which made Tiren's crop flutter eagerly. At least he would not have to worry about starving to death. Those tiny bones and the sparse fabric in which the whole thing was clad would not make for much casting material, but it would be a damned sight better than prison grit and paper and it had been years since Tiren had enjoyed fresh meat. He worried for a second that the little thing might be poisonous but with his hunger gnawing at his insides he did not feel like waiting to find out. As the little creature twitched and fell silent he popped it into his beak and swallowed.

Oh. Oh, yes. His crop demanded more.

The second one squealed even louder as he dragged it from beneath his foot and threw it alive into his mouth. It went down well in spite of all its wiggling. Tiren closed his eyes and savored the desperate flopping in his crop for as long as it lasted before the clenching muscles finally crushed his meal into submission. While he waited for any signs of cramps or hallucinations he studied the dwelling from which his tasty but meager dinner had emerged. It was not very sturdy and came apart easily in his hands. From the contents he deduced that the little creatures possessed only rudimentary technology. What little they had seemed wasted on something so tiny and weak. It was likely that there was nothing larger than they were on the whole of the planet; if there had been, it would have eaten them all into extinction years ago.

And if that were true, then it meant that there was a good chance that Tiren was the biggest living thing in the entire world.

Intrigued by the notion, Tiren turned toward the gray pall on the horizon where he had earlier spotted the tightest concentration of dwellings. There was still a chance that he had misjudged the size of whatever lived there, but if it turned out to be the same little creatures that he had discovered here, then he would have enough food to last a lifetime.

His crop gave a greedy flutter. Tensing his legs he beat his wings down hard and launched himself skyward, then made for the nearest thermal that rose in the direction of the cluster.

It was a city all right, no different from any other on any planet except for its diminutive size. The structures were larger than those he had encountered when he had first landed but, as he discovered with cruel delight, just as fragile. He swooped low, marveling at how readily the flimsy constructs shattered beneath the simple draft from his wings. As his shadow raced across the grid below it sent the puny meatbugs scurrying. Their terror was intoxicating, their flight bringing out the predator in him. They were helpless before him – him! Tiren, the biggest badass their world had ever seen. "That's right! Run!" he bellowed. "You'll all be whitewash by morning!"

He landed feet-first on a pair of boxy structures and rode them down as they crumbled satisfyingly beneath him. Stepping from the rubble he raised all of his feathers and shook the dust from them, then turned a scornful eye to the puny creatures that swarmed below. Their stumbling and squeaking made him roar with laughter and he leaned down, scooping up ten or more at a time with just a sweep of his hand. The sound they made as they flailed in his grip was like sweet music; their wiggling made his crop quiver in eager anticipation. "You ought to be proud," he cooed to them. "You get to be my first full meal here." With that he threw his head back, gaped wide and dropped them all together into his mouth. He waited with his eyes closed, letting them writhe about in his beak before he began to swallow them one and two at a time, moaning in delight as their struggles traveled down his throat and settled in his crop.

The swarm had moved away when he opened his eyes again. "Oh, no you don't," he growled. It took only four steps for him to catch up to them. His hand cleared a wide swath through their midst and bore another squeaking dozen to his mouth. He savored them the same way, then gave in to his belly's insistent pangs and began to cram them into his beak as fast as he could snatch them up. He gulped down a dozen more, then a hundred, a thousand, until his crop bulged heavier than it had since his conviction. Even though he had gorged himself he was pleased to see that there were still millions left. "This is paradise," he cackled, "and it's all mine."

Something impacted against his left arm and he became aware of a popping noise from somewhere below. Swallowing his last mouthful and paying no heed to the two who tumbled from his beak, he scanned the street below and noticed an obstacle that was splitting the stream of retreating prey in half. He had never seen anything quite like it although the colorful dancing lights perched atop it were all too familiar. Leaning closer, he spied two of the tiny creatures crouched in the shelter of its leeward side. The popping was coming from them. "So this is what passes for cops here," he laughed. Whatever they were throwing at him was not doing much good. He could see the impacts ruffling on the surface of his feathers like the patter of rain, but that was all. "You're putting me on," he snickered. "Is that all you've got?"

The little cops stumbled backward as Tiren reached down and seized what was no doubt their cruiser in one hand. "I'll tell you, Boys," he said casually, "Your kind make damned fine eating. The only problem, though, is that you don't give a guy much to cast afterward." Bringing the cruiser to his beak he bit down and tore it in two. "Those little bones, that thin skin..." He paused to swallow the front half of the wreck. "...it's just not healthy. For me, that is." He threw the rest of the cruiser into his maw and gulped it down as well. "Meat is fine, but a fellow really needs to be able to cough up a good, firm pellet after a big meal."

Pop-pop, pop-pop! More pattering on his chest. Something the size of a grain of sand left a thin scrape on the side of his beak. Another hit the nictitating membrane of his left eye, doing no damage but irritating the hell out of him. "That's it!" he snarled. Standing tall, he raised all of his feathers and flared his wings to their full span, casting a hellishly enormous shadow on the swarm. "I'm going to teach you fucking insects your proper place!"

The police tried to retreat but were caught up in the swarm. Like a living river the mob spun the officers around and carried them with it while overhead a glaring Tiren lifted his foot. "This is how we kill bugs where I come from," he growled, and stamped down hard, deliberately missing the cops but crushing a huge number of their nearby kin. He made a great show of lifting his foot and holding it aloft so that the cops could get a good look at the dozens of corpses mashed against its underside. With a flex of his toes he made a slab of raw meat peel off and batter down on them in chunks. He stomped again, then with his other foot, then with the first, purposefully avoiding the tiny blue-clad figures while trampling the bodies around them into mush, and all the while laughing raucously. Eventually the cops stood alone in a field of flattened citizens with Tiren glaring down at them.

Pop-pop-pop-pop, and his feathers ruffled all over his body. More of the little bastards were coming out of the woodwork. Tiren snorted. "I was wondering when you were going to get around to sending backup," he said to the two below. With one foot he swiped at them, gutting them both with a single claw before turning to the newcomers. "Well, here I am!" he gloated, spreading his arms and wings out wide. "So what are you waiting for? Arrest me, you little fuckers."

The popping was nearly constant now and the feathers of Tiren's chest and belly were dancing as though in a strong wind. Bits of metallic sand rained down from his body as he advanced slowly upon the police line, one blood-caked foot after another, fixing the cops in his malevolent gaze until he stood right over them. The popping abruptly stopped and the cops bolted but they did not get very far. Tiren's hand easily overtook them, plowing them all together before closing around the entire kicking mass and lifting them skyward. Leering, Tiren slowly sat down, flattening one of their cruisers beneath his rump and catching the ghost of a final scream from the vehicle's occupants.

They squealed like tiny rodents when Tiren held them close to his eyes. The idea of police officers being so tiny that he could grip them in one hand was an unimaginable thrill. "Are you begging?" he said to them. He clenched his fist just a little, just enough to make them squeal even louder. "You should be. I could crush you all right now. All I have to do is squeeze – oh, yeah, I'd love to do that." His hand relaxed slightly. "But no. You little fucks are going to suffer."

He was interrupted by a sharp pain on his left buttock. "Ow! Shit!" Leaning to his right he raised his cheek and brushed at the feathers. He wondered for a moment if someone had somehow survived in the flattened cruiser and had managed to get off a lucky shot, but from between two of his feathers emerged a miniscule creature about the size of a feather-mite. It was a bizarre thing with four tiny legs and a thin tail and two angular points on its furry head, which Tiren figured must be what it used to suck his blood. "You little piece of filth," he growled, snatching up an undamaged cruiser and hurling it at the mite as it darted away. It skittered from side to side, dodging the tumbling vehicle before darting out of sight.

Tiren rubbed ruefully at his rump and then returned his attention to his captives. "You call yourselves police?" he grumbled, his voice rasping with contempt. "You're pathetic! A fucking little parasite just got in a better shot on me than any of you."

Of course they did not understand what he was saying, the mindless little pricks, and that annoyed him even more. He decided that a demonstration was in order. Dragging one of them from his grip with his other hand he flipped it up and caught one of its legs in his beak. A casual twist of his head: Rip! The leg disappeared down his throat as the little thing wailed. The other leg was next: Rip! Then an arm.

By then his victim had stopped making noise. Tiren shrugged, tossed the rest into his mouth and gulped. The display seemed to have had the desired effect on the rest of the captives who were writhing more frantically than ever. Tiren clicked his beak and marveled out loud, "Whoa...I just ate a cop!" He lifted the struggling officers very close to his eyes and narrowed his gaze. "And I'm going to eat a lot more, believe me. But first, it's Payback Time."

He transferred one cop to his left foot, curling the long toes around in a firm grip, and two to his right. The remaining four he clutched together in his fist while rubbing into the feathers of his groin with his other hand. With the rush from having such ultimate control over a handful of police it did not take long for him to make himself hard. "What do you think of that?" he taunted as he held them in the shadow of the mighty shaft which loomed over them like a building. They gibbered, cowering; Tiren was convinced that they were pleading for mercy, which only stoked his urges. Opening his hand he cupped it quickly around his erection, squeezing the puny cops against it. A shudder ran through him and he began to pant. Their voices rose to a shrill whine as he began to jerk his hand roughly up and down, dragging them in brutal strokes along the fleshy spire.

It did not take long. Tiren came hard, harder than he had in years, his spunk shooting almost as high as his head. He gripped tightly with his fingers, quivering at the feeling of the cops being crushed to death against his spurting shaft, their subjugation complete. Gasping, he lay back against the building behind him and continued to stroke himself until the very last spasm had passed. All that was left of the police by now were red tatters that hung, cum-draped, from his fingers. He flicked them away and sighed blissfully.

By now the street around him was deserted. Tiren gathered the remaining captives back into one hand and addressed them loftily. "So where are all your people?" he asked. "Hiding, I imagine. That's fine. I'll hunt them down as soon as I'm hungry again. As for you..." He held them close again. "...I'm keeping you. I've got some ideas that I'm sure you aren't going to like one bit."

One of them howled. Smirking, Tiren stuffed the tip of a claw into the tiny mouth, silencing the cries, and he laughed coldly. "You know, back home, your kind just couldn't resist being up my ass. I think that tomorrow you three are going to get to find out what that's like."

Tiren squawked with laughter and stood up quickly. Right away he noticed that something was wrong. The buildings around him wobbled and the ground made a sudden lurch that dropped him to his knees. The cops fell forgotten from his hand. He sat down hard. "My head..." he groaned. "What the hell? Are you little bastards poisoned after all?" He blinked away an annoying haze. His arm felt like rock when he reached up to rub at his brow. Every joint throbbed painfully.

Relax.

"What?" Tiren rubbed at his eyes and peered all around.

Relax, I said.

He felt the need to empty his crop. "Who the hell is saying that?"

Down here.

Tiren squinted and peered at the ground before him. He saw nothing at first, but then through the gathering fog he made out the diminutive shape of a mite, and a closer look convinced him that it was the very same one that had bitten him earlier. It was not darting away this time, but rather sat serenely preening at a cluster of tiny whiskers that sprouted from its snout. For a moment it busied itself with licking at a forelimb and rubbing it over its face before it lifted its head to meet Tiren's gaze. *You know, we hunt and kill your kind for sport on this world, although I confess that I have never before seen one your size. It surprises me all the more that my bite would affect you so quickly. Who would have imagined that you would be so weak?*

"How the hell...how can you be talking to me?"

How indeed? The mite curled its thin tail around its haunches. *Your mind is receptive, at least on a very basic level.*

Tiren felt feverish. It took nearly all of his strength to raise his fist and bring it crashing down upon the annoying pest, but the mite sprang aside at the last instant and peered balefully at him. *I told you to relax. You're only making it harder on yourself.*

"What did you do to me?"

The tiny creature sat down and twisted its head around to wash its back. *What a silly question. I have killed you, of course.*

Tiren's mouth fell open. The mite finished washing its back, then yawned and settled down to its belly. *The bacteria in my saliva usually does its work within days. You must be particularly sensitive to it. Lie still, now. The less you move, the faster you will die.*

"You little bastard. What the hell did I ever do to you?"

Do? You were butchering our slaves. We could not have that, now, could we?

"Slaves?" Tiren's beak sagged down to his chest. "You mean...?"

Naturally. Those creatures belong to us. They are a servant species, dull and brutish but not without their uses. You did not honestly think for a moment that something like them could be the dominant species on this world, did you?

Another mite appeared, then two more, then a dozen, a hundred, a thousand, creeping from the depths of the rubble and surrounding him. Their tiny glowing eyes were the last thing he saw before his own eyes closed and he could not open them any longer. "You could have just told me," he wheezed.

Would it have stopped you? No, I don't think so. You have to eat, after all. The mite licked briefly over its nose and added, *as, of course, do we.*

Tiren could only groan in reply. He felt himself slipping away. A pinprick sent a jolt of pain through his haunch, followed by another, then a dozen, a hundred, a thousand. *There's quite a lot of you to go around. I suspect we will only have time for the choicest parts before our servants return to finish the job. Even so, let me say that your meat is far tastier than your smaller local brethren.*

You ought to be proud.

The Holocene Extinction

It is a perverse irony that we, Mankind, tended to define geographic eras by the periodic and mysterious mass extinctions that we discovered in the fossil record. Species flourished for thousands of years, millions of years, and then in the blink of a cosmic eye they vanished. With every ghostly echo of cataclysm that we found in the rocks we started time over again and gave it a new name. The Triassic Period, the Jurassic, the Cretaceous, and then the less spectacular (to all, perhaps, except those who perished) Oligocene and Pleistocene all came and went. Each ended abruptly, dozens of species swept all at once from the face of the earth. Theories abounded, of course, everything from volcanoes to climate changes to comet impacts, but nobody could ever say for certain why. People kept arguing the point right up until our own era came to an end. Understanding of the true cause of those great extinctions finally came about with our own.

We called our epoch the Holocene, those hundred or so centuries since human beings first started to use primitive tools. It ended with the arrival of a being that I have come to call Talos after the indestructible giant of Greek myth whose story can be found in one of the books that I shall soon be sealing away along with this narrative. I have imagined him moving from world to world, returning now and again to see what might have grown back since his last visit, like a farmer harvesting apples from a tree year after year. I am certain that our ancient ancestors must have witnessed him feasting upon the mastodon and the titanothere and kept the images alive in a racial memory that, as we grew, we began to dismiss as fanciful legend. Those ancestors survived doubtless because they were beneath his notice at the time – too small, too few alongside the meatier and more plentiful beasts. Talos left them alone then, but upon his return he found that they had prospered, grown ripe for the picking, and unlike his mythical namesake there was no vein in his ankle to be opened, no Medea to rise and save us.

The final days of the Holocene were signaled by the annihilation of Shanghai in the People's Republic of China. Nearly ten million voices literally went silent one day when without warning all communications from the city ceased. No radio signals. No computer traffic. Telephone conversations were cut off in mid-word. It was as if a great curtain had been drawn in an instant around the city. The Chinese were a secretive people and distrustful of outsiders, and thus they greeted all inquiries from abroad with a curt dismissal. A power failure, they said, and nothing more. All was well.

The next day, however, foreign satellites spied a massive plume of smoke rising from the region. Normal optics could not penetrate it; curiously, even the heat sensing eyes of the military revealed only a featureless red haze. The offerings of assistance from abroad became increasingly urgent but were only met with indignation by the Chinese government. It was two weeks before the smoke began to clear and the infrared cameras hovering over the region could finally see again. They revealed to a stunned world a smoldering, blighted landscape. Of the ten million inhabitants not one could be found alive.

Finally the government grudgingly confessed that "something of a grave catastrophe" had taken place, but rather than asking for help they began to hurl accusations at their rivals. Rescue crews that had charged into the smoke had vanished without a trace as had military units who followed, save for a few dazed survivors who stumbled from the ruins with reports that every piece of electrical equipment in their possession had inexplicably failed. Radios went silent, vehicles sputtered to a halt, leaving the teams to grope their way blindly back to their staging areas. Most did not make it. The Chinese concluded that an enemy state had launched a sneak attack on Shanghai with an atomic weapon. Their politicians cried out for vengeance and threatened to mobilize their army. Diplomats from all over the world appealed to them to be calm, pointing out that nowhere could a trace of radioactivity be detected, neither from the ground nor from space, so it was quite improbable that a nuclear device had been detonated. Wouldn't China allow foreign scientists the chance to examine the remains of some of the victims to determine what had happened to them?

The bitter reply: "We cannot find any!"

The end might have come very quickly as tempers flared and all parties began to prepare for war had not a similar tragedy befallen Seoul in South Korea. A city almost as large as Shanghai, Seoul disappeared the same way, first into silence, and then beneath a black and impenetrable cloud. Military and news media rushed to the scene only to find their sophisticated equipment rendered useless, their aircraft falling helplessly from the sky. Breathless reports from observers near the outskirts of the city told of great shrieking crowds and tumbling buildings, of fires and of "something moving" before their voices faded into the static.

There was nothing that could be done. Mankind's great technological and military might was powerless against this mysterious weapon.

Nearly everyone who ventured into the choking haze never came out again. A very few, however, returned wide-eyed and screaming and babbling barely coherent tales of giant monsters stalking through the streets. Naturally these were discounted but only at first, for the few ragged and stunned survivors that began to stagger toward the military perimeter all stammered out the same fantastic story. One even managed to scrawl a picture of a black demonic shape before collapsing in convulsions and dying. The rest were spirited away to secure locations, but not before their stories were flashed in news reports around the world, touching off an international panic. Riots broke out in many major cities and had to be quelled by police and local militia. Politicians berated their citizenry for giving in to hysteria and listening to the ravings of a few poor souls who had been driven to insanity by some unimaginable trauma.

Monster or weapon, it left nothing of Seoul behind but a burning wasteland. TV cameras swarmed over the rubble the very moment Mankind's expensive toys started to work again. They found not one building left intact, just acres of pulverized wreckage. Scientists diligently searched for a blast pattern; they found none. They hunted for chemical residues and quickly discovered enormous levels of iridium in the ashes. Some argued that this was certainly evidence of a meteor impact, or perhaps even a cluster similar to the impact that (they believed) had snuffed out the great dinosaurs. The theory was denounced by others who asked how a meteor strike could leave behind so few survivors and even fewer bodies. More visionary thinkers concentrated on deep craters beneath the rubble that looked suspiciously like footprints. The survivors' wild tales would seem to support that conclusion, and that was the first time that the name of Talos was invoked in the tabloid headlines.

The debate was positively savage. For every great thinker who held that the evidence pointed to a giant living creature as the cause of the destruction there was an equally great thinker who pointed out that creatures of such size could not simply evaporate into thin air when they were through. Conspiracy theories abounded, such as one that claimed that the monster stories had been created by a sinister corporate conglomerate to hide their plans for employing nuclear suicide bombers to destroy all but a few key centers of commerce. Religious zealots proclaimed that the Almighty was punishing mankind for his sins and that only the righteous would be saved while the rest would be doomed to extinction.

I laughed at them along with everyone else who never imagined that the zealots were closest to the truth. I became a believer on the day that the force of extinction turned its hungry eye upon the city where I lived and worked. It was on that day that I along with the millions of souls around me would cower before the might of Talos.

His arrival was heralded by a clap of thunder that drew me to my window. I was puzzled by such noise from a sky that held no hint of rain. The clouds were white and billowy, but then an odd thing caught my eye. Overhead there was a disturbance, a great swirling and spinning of the cloud mass. It looked to me like water draining from a tub. The center of the spiral turned black and crackled with lightning, then all at once drew in on itself and formed a shape. Huge wings beat the surrounding clouds into froth as behind me the desk lamp faded and the computer sighed into silence.

Talos had come.

I stood dumbfounded as he descended upon the city, his titanic body swallowing the light as it loomed larger and larger, dwarfing the great skyscrapers below it. One wing dropped and he banked, swooping across the dome of the sky. A wave of white-hot energy burst from his maw, kindling the buildings instantly into flame in a miles-long swath beneath him. He rose at the end and spun about, wings beating to a hover. I could see him clearly then, a living shadow, a dragon more terrible, more unbelievable to behold than any storybook creation. His gaze swept from side to side at the expanse of the city below him and I saw his long tongue slither out of his jaws and sweep up over his lips, and then he furled his wings and dropped.

A nearby grocery store where I used to buy my food was crushed instantly as a foot larger than a house landed upon it. The dragon's hind legs flexed momentarily beneath the impact before he rose to his full height, towering even over the bank building on the corner. That whole structure had gone dark, even its garish rooftop sign extinguished by the peculiar energy which I understood at that moment was a part of the monster's being. Talos gazed down upon its forty stories of concrete and steel for only a moment, and then with an air of contempt he placed a mighty hand upon its façade and shoved it aside as casually as a man might push aside a sapling standing in his path.

Someone seized me by the arm and tore me away from the window seconds before it exploded inward. There followed a wild jumble of dark corridors, of rushing bodies and my feet stumbling down endless flights of stairs. I remember being swept into the street in a veritable wave of humanity, many of them falling into a tangled pile just outside the doors. I do not know how I managed to escape being trampled as the crowd carried me along with it. Dazed, I looked up to where the dragon had stood and saw only the dazzlingly bright sky. That sight itself was disorienting. The sky had always been hidden behind the bank building, which just like Talos had disappeared into thin air. In its place was a mountain of twisted puzzle-pieces, of brick and masonry from which dust and curls of smoke rose all over.

The upper floors of the building which I had just vacated suddenly exploded into a blinding ball of orange fire. The roar of the flames drowned out the screams of those around me as the city's population became a human river sweeping me down the street. It was an endless battle simply to stay on one's feet. Those who fell were dead within seconds. Later, I would envy them.

The fires seemed to follow us at every turn. The mob's numbers swelled as untold hundreds poured in shrieking waves from doorways while smoke billowed behind them and rubble rained down from the heavens. I could not see where I was or where I was being carried. My mind was occupied only with keeping myself from drowning in the sea of panicked men and women.

I recall briefly seeing the morning sun framed in the broad avenue ahead of me before it was suddenly snuffed out. In its place a leg rose before me, and quickly a second strode into view. Each stood as tall as a skyscraper, twin towers of muscle sheathed in volcanic rock. I raised my eyes, higher, higher. I could not hear the shouts of those around me. I could not even hear my own scream of terror. There was only the sound of my own heartbeat thudding in my ears.

Talos stood in our path, upright, his tail snaking behind him into the smoke-filled distance, his head lowered toward us. His blazing eyes glittered as they shifted slowly, playing over the thousands of shocked, upturned faces far below. They were not the cold and mindless eyes of a reptile that I would have expected, no, not at all. Those eyes were thoughtful and cunning and seared into me with a malevolence that was almost as physical a presence as the dragon himself. The monster's lips drew back from glittering white teeth. That sneer held a depth of scorn that was made sickeningly clear with the raising of a mammoth foot. It shifted slowly forward, just a little, just enough to cast those closest to him in its shadow.

And then he stepped on them. Just like that.

They vanished beneath his foot with a red splash. My hearing returned with the sound of their bodies being pressed flat, followed by a deafening shriek of terror from the crowd. The jostling and clawing became frantic around me, shredding my jacket and tie to tatters in an instant. On all sides people were struggling to turn themselves around, their minds blindly fixated on fleeing from the danger even though the crush of people around them made it impossible to move either forward or backward. The gigantic foot rose ponderously, casting more of us in its shadow as it swept forward. A steady shower of pulverized pavement and bits of raw meat rained down upon our faces.

It did not fall, but rather hung tormentingly in the sky above us. I could clearly see the pitifully tiny outlines of bodies dotting the vast underside. There seemed to be hundreds of them, all twisted into grotesque shapes, each mashed as flat as paper and stuck to the gargantuan sole by a crimson paste. The great foot began to swing slowly from side to side, shifting the awful spectacle over first one part of the crowd and then another, taunting us.

Those behind me were pushing hard, squeezing the breath from me. Seconds before I would have suffocated from the pressure the people before me lurched forward. The mob had at last managed to reverse its direction and had begun its ponderous retreat. I saw the shadow of the dragon's toes disappear as I fought my way forward, and behind me a hundred voices rose into a piercing squeal. Glancing over my shoulder I saw the gigantic foot coming down. Its vast bulk settled with agonizing slowness onto their heads, pushing them down into a huddle and then covering them. The huge toes settled last of all, the tips of their talons digging into the pavement as if into a sandy beach. The toes shifted apart as the dragon's weight came to bear on them and a hideous crunching noise filled the air. I could see a few pathetic survivors jerking and kicking beneath. The foot twisted slowly from side to side, a deliberate act that brutally rolled the survivors beneath it for an agonizing second before grinding their bodies into hamburger. A few seconds later the foot rose again into the sky, and I could not bear to look at what was left.

Talos watched the desperate struggling from on high with cold amusement, then raised his head to the heavens and let loose a roar of laughter. He *laughed!* That sound, which I still can hear in my sleep, made it plain that that this was no brainless animal acting on instinct. This was a malignant force, the very embodiment of cruelty, a monster who before my eyes had just deliberately snuffed out countless lives purely for amusement. Moreover, I realized with a jolt of renewed panic that this monster had been herding us – was still herding us, in fact. His steps were short and deliberate, and we were fleeing from the crushing weight of his tread exactly as he intended us to.

With a jarring crash our tormentor dropped to all fours behind us, his saurian head swaying slowly to and fro as he regarded our wild flight.

His eyes narrowed with satisfaction at the sea of humanity continuing its sluggish retreat before him. I wanted desperately to call out to my fellow citizens not to let themselves be driven into a trap but such an effort was beyond hopeless. I could do nothing but flee with the rest of the herd and try to survive as best I could. Behind us Talos waited, peering about for a moment with apparent disinterest before taking a single thundering step that instantly closed the distance we had gained. His forefoot rose and slashed, sending broken bodies cartwheeling over our heads to smack into the walls on either side of us, again and again. In this fashion he drove us onward, the crowd blindly obeying their terrible master and fighting their way through the burning canyon in a great shrieking mass.

And then, alas, there was nowhere left to go. A mountain of rubble lay before us, hell fires licking out from countess broken window frames across its face. Crumbling, smoking buildings formed impenetrable walls to either side. The crowd behind me continued to push, immobilizing me once again in its painful embrace.

Talos approached on all fours behind us with his lazy, deliberate pace. Slowly he sat down, his haunches forming a wall across the street as impenetrable as those around us. For a moment he studied us with cool indifference, and then his nightmarish head descended, snaking toward us upon its long neck. The people fought to retreat but were so tightly packed into the makeshift corral that they could do nothing more than jerk their heads and scream as the dragon's nose hovered above, drawing in great draughts of breath and blowing back out violently. He sniffed them casually, examining, pondering....

...deciding.

His muzzle rose slightly and from between the inky black lips slipped a long, long tongue, its surface glistening with firelight reflected from above. It thrust itself down into the thick of the crowd and writhed in their midst. When it rose again I could see a large number of kicking figures surrounded in its coiled length and being hauled skyward. Yet more were stuck oddly to its wet surface, their limbs dancing and flailing but never pulling free. The great jaws parted, flashing the tips of white fangs and echoing with a contented rumble. The dragon's tongue slithered inside, dragging the helpless victims along with it. His lips closed behind them and he swallowed, an enormous lump rolling smoothly down the length of his throat. Briefly his eyes closed and he was motionless, savoring the struggles of his prey within him. When his eyes opened again they gleamed with cruel delight, and his tongue dipped down for more.

I cannot say how many hundreds, if not thousands of my fellow human beings I saw being eaten alive that day. The awful tongue thrust forth again and again, snatching people up in great clumps and pulling them, squealing and pleading pathetically, into the dragon's mouth to be swallowed whole. Our corral became the scene of a hellish fight for survival as people began to claw at one another, literally tearing their neighbors apart in order to avoid being licked up like ants. As Talos fed, the crowd thinned steadily so that ultimately there was room enough for us to move about, and we did, rushing this way and that in a frantic bid for survival. The great tongue chased after us, at one point sweeping close enough to me that one of its struggling victims was able to reach out and seize my arm in a death grip. I was hoisted into the air and in utter panic I flipped upward and broke the grasping arm like a twig over my knee. Freed, I fell to the pavement and watched as the man's despairing face vanished behind the dragon's teeth.

Talos swallowed that mouthful and then raised his haunches and shifted them forward in order to shrink the corral. He would have sat on me had I not managed to scramble to my feet and dart out of his way. As I ran I felt the warmth radiating from his tongue and I threw myself down to the pavement. Tons of wet, pink muscle snaked within inches of me and then withdrew, carrying with it a fresh, squalling catch. Some who were left behind were now grabbing at those nearby and shoving, pushing them up toward the dragon's tongue in a barbaric attempt to win a few more seconds of life by sacrificing their neighbors. I got up again and ran blindly, dodging where I could, punching and kicking at those who would try to feed me to the dragon ahead of themselves. Talos lapped at the areas where the crowd was thickest, but as our numbers grew ever thinner he began to chase us with his hands, gathering us up in clawed fingers and tossing us casually into his mouth like living popcorn.

Raw terror has left me with mercifully little memory of the next few moments. I do know that I was caught once but managed to wriggle free, a sharp talon-tip ripping what was left of my shirt from my body. I remember leaping and ducking, dodging both the dragon's hand and the other fear-crazed people trapped with me, over and over and over, until suddenly there was nowhere left to run. I found myself backed against the barrier of rubble that Talos had used to entrap us. The concrete chunks were glowing hot from the fires that burned beneath and seared my skin as I tried to cower against them. Talos loomed above, gazing almost straight down at me. Other than myself there was no one left between the dragon's haunches and the fiery walls. The corral was empty, but oddly I could still hear the wailing of countless voices, muffled and dissonant. The sound was much like that from a distant football stadium when a touchdown was made, and strange as it may seem I remember thinking, "How could they be playing a game at a time like this?" Then with a horror that cannot be described in words I realized that the cries were coming from within the dragon's stomach. Behind that towering wall of muscle and scales they were still alive, struggling, screaming, slowly being digested.

At that moment, mercifully, I fainted.

It might have been days before I awoke again; I do not know. That dreadful sound was still in my ears and I rolled over and was sick. The smoke had settled to a dull gray haze. There was no sign of Talos. I lay where I had fallen for a long time before I gathered the strength to climb to my feet. It took even longer for me to find the courage to inch my way from the corral and out into the remnants of the city.

No. It was not a city any longer. These were not streets. Surrounding me were mountains of debris with twisted girders rising like skeletal fingers from beneath. Great works of man, once proud symbols of creativity and skill, had all toppled like children's sandcastles. I began to stumble among the remains, terrorized now and then by a nearby roar and crash. Certain that the dragon was returning to finish me off I would hide, only to discover that the noise had come from weakened buildings that finally succumbed to the battering they had suffered. Fire was everywhere, and so were the bodies, or what little was left. I could not walk more than a few yards without finding the remains of some poor soul squashed flat against the ground. Seagulls and crows were already quarrelling over them. As I passed by them the birds fussed and glowered at me but did not fly away. It was almost as though they, too, now held my kind in disdain.

I came at last to a great pile of wreckage that stretched high over my head and into the hazy distance to either side. I began to work my way around it but then paused, noticing something unusual. A collapsing building will leave behind a mound of girders and concrete. Those things I could plainly see in the rubble before me, but also here and there was a mangled vehicle. I suspected at first that I was looking at the remains of a parking garage, but then I saw mailboxes and light posts tangled amidst the wreckage and realized that this mountain of debris had not come about by a simple collapse. It had been piled there.

Hope welled up in me. This could only mean that the onslaught had ended and that the sad cleanup had begun. I was sure to find an army of workers on the other side wearily shoveling through the wreckage and adding it to the pile as they searched for survivors. "I'm here!" I shouted. With salvation in reach I leaped up onto a jagged piece of masonry and began to climb. It was a painful ascent. Shards of glass bit into my fingers but I did not care. Pieces of wreckage shifted crazily beneath me but I did not stop climbing. I had no other thought in my head but for reaching the top.

At last, nearly exhausted, I grasped the bumper of a flattened sportscar with a bleeding hand and hauled myself up to the summit. There I let out a whoop of joy and staggered forward to wave to my rescuers, only to feel that hope come crashing down like the buildings behind me. Below was a wide, empty clearing, its further end obscured by a black wall of smoke. It was obvious that the wreckage had been purposefully swept from that area to form the ridge upon which I was now perched, but no workmen were in sight, nor was there any sign of heavy machinery. The inner walls of the enclosure were much steeper than the slope I had just climbed, making descent that way impossible...

Descent...or ascent.

My gut froze. I suddenly realized that I had seen this sort of thing before.

Then I heard screams.

It began as a faint siren-wail in the distance but quickly rose in volume. From the smoky pall a few rushing figures emerged, followed right away by a veritable torrent of humanity pouring into the clearing. Those at the forefront tried to stop as they recognized that they had fled into a dead end; they were pushed down instantly and overrun as the human tide flowed over them. It took only seconds for the enclosure below to fill with people, all packing themselves in tightly and forming a shifting, struggling mass. I wished that I could reach down to snatch even one of them up with me to safety.

Inevitably, from the veil of smoke in the distance, Talos appeared.

I froze, clinging wide-eyed and helpless to the wreckage. The dragon's head swayed slowly from side to side, peering down at the tiny creatures that fled before him, just as he had done when I myself had been among his intended victims. Bit by bit his long neck emerged from the smoke, his shoulders fading into view, and I watched as his head dropped down. His tongue swept up dozens of running figures and drew them into his mouth. His eyes narrowed to contented slits and his jaw began working, chewing them. Huge chunks of crimson meat fell from his lips and landed on those fleeing below, knocking them down. The awful sight drove the crowd mad with fear and sent them blindly rushing forward, exactly as Talos knew it would.

The number of people rushing out of the smoke dwindled while behind them the dragon continued his patient advance, his forelegs and broad chest appearing. He peered dispassionately at the sea of humans who were now helpless before him, and then once again he loosed that hideous laugh and advanced into the very thick of the crowd. He ignored those who were crushed beneath his feet as he lumbered forward, and as soon as his hind feet landed amongst those at the rear of the enclosure he callously sat upon them, sealing the trap in a dreadfully familiar fashion. My stomach lurched to see so many tiny hands thrusting upward in such a pitiful effort to ward off their doom before they disappeared.

Thousands were now trapped just as I had once been and I could not help them. I could not even move for fear that the dragon would notice me and flick me down into the enclosure to suffer the fate that I had previously escaped. I could only stare as the unbearable scene played out before me.

To have only devoured them would have been appalling, but what he did instead staggers the civilized mind. For some time Talos paid no attention to the screeching mob below him and merely sat regally. At one point he even twisted his head about to nibble at an annoying itch on his back before returning his cold gaze to the captives. I noticed with revulsion then that he had become hideously aroused. A monstrous penis, bigger than a bus, stood forth from his haunches and loomed ominously over those struggling beneath. Even before I could fully grasp what was happening he reached forth with a foreclaw, scooped a great mass of flailing bodies beneath him and – god help me – used them to pleasure himself. Used them! I can still hear the terrible sounds they made as they were crushed to death, sacrificed to the dragon's obscene pleasure. Unsatisfied with the frailty of the first handful the dragon reached for more, and then again, and yet again, squashing them over and over by the handful.

I felt lightheaded, sick with dread and with rising anger. Yes, anger. In a perverse sense I believe I could accept the fate of humanity to be preyed upon by a more powerful being, a fate which our kind had unwittingly been spared for countless centuries but which is the inevitable destiny of all creatures in nature. What I was witness to, however, was not predation. It was sport.

The slaughter went on and on as the dragon continued to amuse himself with his captives, until finally he loosed a roar that shook the air around me and his climax burst forth in a deadly geyser that crashed through the survivors like a liquid missile. Many were dashed to pieces against the wall below me by the force of the stream; others nearby were mired in the thick slime and quickly suffocated. Another blast roared through the crowd, killing hundreds. It was followed by another, and another, and another, each more powerful than the last and cutting a different course, catching fresh victims in its path as Talos turned his orgasm into a cruel and murderous game.

Eventually the torrents subsided and Talos released his enormous member with a groan. It seemed surprising to him that some of his playthings had survived. They huddled, whimpering and sobbing out desperate prayers, at the base of the wall directly below me. Talos eyed them and then rose, arched his back in a colossal stretch, and stalked forward. I cringed as his head loomed over me and uttered my own prayers that I would not be spotted. I watched as he settled once again and entertained himself for a time with the remaining victims, scooping them away from the wall with his claws and hurling them one at a time into the pools of his seed before popping them under his thumb. He soon grew bored with that game, however, and seizing all of the survivors at once he swept them with both hands into a squirming pile before him. Rising to his hind legs, he turned full around and squatted over them, and then in a disgusting display of contempt he raised his tail and buried them in the steaming remains of those whom he had previously devoured.

My gorge rose. Talos turned again and dropped to all fours, and then with a mighty foreclaw he raked at the wall of rubble and brought it tumbling down atop his waste. The car to which I was clinging shuddered and began to topple forward. With a wild cry I let go of the bumper and scrambled for a handhold in the shifting debris but found none. The entire mountain was collapsing into the pit and carrying me along with it.

I landed on a hard surface that knocked the wind out of me. I had resigned myself to being pulverized by the avalanche of debris but after a few seconds passed I realized that I was being held aloft even while tumbling bricks and glass shards cascaded downward before me. I felt that I was rising higher into the air. I saw a forest of claws jutting skyward before me, felt warmth beneath my body.

I knew where I was, and surprisingly I was not at all afraid. What good is fear, after all, when you are lying in the palm of a dragon's hand? I felt calm, and in fact almost exhilarated. How foolish I had been! All of that wasted effort to survive only to prolong the inevitable. All of it had been a game which Talos had just won. Smiling with that notion I turned myself around and gazed straight up into the dragon's eyes. "Tag!" I called gleefully. "You're it!"

He made no movement other than a flaring of his nostrils. We stared at one another and before long I became annoyed. "Well?" I shouted. "What's the hold up?" Climbing to my feet, I snatched up a small piece of brick that had fallen into his hand along with me. "What, am I not amusing enough for you? Come on, let's get it over with. I'm sick of it, and frankly, I'm sick of you."

He did not budge. Angrily I hurled the chunk of brick as hard as I could against the muzzle looming over me. "What's the matter? Oh, oh, wait. I get it. You're the god, right? I forgot about that. What's it going to be, then? Am I righteous enough for you, or am I just another sinner?"

My ears rang with a growl that rolled like a thunder. The hand shifted violently beneath me, throwing me off my feet. I landed with a grunt and tried to sit up but the dragon's palm tilted sharply, spilling me off and sending me rolling helplessly onto the ground.

When my vision cleared the dragon was nowhere in sight. I was left alone in a lifeless city.

That was almost ten years ago. I have not seen another living human being for the last four. Some might be in hiding but I do not think it likely. One cannot hide from extinction. I've seen great canyons left behind after Talos has dug them out of their shelters. I suppose that if there are any others left alive on other continents that they are afraid to gather in any sizeable groups for fear of attracting his notice. That puts us back to the beginning, back to the first days of the Holocene when we were few, feeble and nomadic, and cowering like we do today in a giant's shadow.

Every day I ask myself why I was spared. Was it cruel whimsy? Did my defiance spark some glimmer of admiration in him, enough to earn me my life? Or was he indeed a god, and I, unwitting and ignorant, one of the righteous? I suppose I shall never know. What I do know is that I may well be the only one left in the world who knows the entire story. Perhaps it is because I am destined to tell the tale that I have been spared.

I do not hold out much hope that my species will survive. Talos's hunger is insatiable and I sadly believe that by the time he has grown weary of this planet and decides to move on to other hunting grounds, there will be too few of us left to thrive. Those of us who were not digested or ground into dust beneath his feet, our bones will be found someday by whoever succeeds us in naming the next era. With luck, this record and the books that accompany it will survive the passage of time and will be found by someone who is able to understand what I have written. My legacy to you is the answer to the question of why a species, why even a great and thriving civilization, can be cast so suddenly into oblivion.

May I humbly suggest, as my final words to posterity, that the era that will dawn with my passing be named the Talosian. It seems only fitting. I wish you peace and prosperity and happiness for all the years that you will enjoy before Talos comes for you as well.

Delusions of Grandeur

So you want to know what happened to the town of Opal, do you? No, I don't think you do. You want to know what I *believe* to have happened. You have your own version, of course, and obviously your version is the correct one, because otherwise you would be the one strapped to a bed with a bag dripping dope into his veins. My version doesn't fit in with your tidy little view of the world, you see, while yours makes all kinds of sense. Mount Rainier, being part of the Ring of Fire that it is, takes a tip from Mount Saint Helens and blasts a few hundred feet off of its peak. The town of Opal is buried in the blink of an eye under sixty feet of mud and volcanic ash, a modern-day Herculaneum, not a single witness, not a single survivor out of all those good people, boo-hoo, boo-hoo.

But you know what? There *was* a witness. There *was* a survivor. The only problem is that his story doesn't jive with what you've already decided is the truth. You have no idea how he came to be wandering naked and raving through the streets of Seattle; all you're sure of is that it couldn't have anything to do with the late, lamented Opal.

Let's make a bet. If I win, you get them to make me up a nice certificate that says "not crazy" on it and let me out of here. Here's what you do: go to that big mud flat you keep telling me about and start digging. Dig three or four holes – no, hell, dig a hundred of them – and if you find so much as a single brick, a single hubcap, a single scrap of newspaper, then I guess I'll spend the rest of my days making bubble-lips with the rest of the lunatics here.

You won't, though. You won't find anything. Not a gum wrapper, not a piece of broken glass, and certainly not any bodies. Why not? Because it's like I told them, *there's nothing under that mud!*

You still want to hear the story? Fine. Just do me a favor: no nodding, no sympathetic smiles, no little whispers of, "oh, dear, isn't that dreadful?" I'm sick to death of getting that. Sit your ass down, shut up, put on your poker face, and listen good.

I've been living in Opal – that is, I *was* living there – for the last four years, ever since I got out of college. It was the prettiest place on Earth, with lots of trees, big hills and valleys to hike around in, and Mount Rainier rising just like a postcard in the distance. It was about the farthest cry from my old stomping grounds in Oklahoma that you can imagine. I had a good job, a nice house that I'd just put a down payment on, and a beautiful big screen television. The only thing I've been lacking of late is a girlfriend, but that's a different story, and it was a mutual thing so you can't point to that as some sort of trigger for "profound detachment from reality."

Anyway.

I'd gone out jogging, just like I did every morning. I got into the habit back in school and never got out of it, which is how I've managed to keep fit when the fellows I went to high school with are all starting to get guts. Mount Rainier was smoking, but then, it had been smoking for almost six months. We were all getting used to the tremors and such. Everyone had read the pamphlets they put out and we all knew the difference between the types of alerts and what to do and when to get ourselves out of there. The mountain had been so quiet of late that that very morning they had downgraded to an "advisory." That pretty much means, "Hey, there's a mountain over there and one of these days it might explode."

Don't you think it's suspicious that all this would have happened when the mountain's activity was supposedly at its lowest?

So I went out jogging before work. Just like any other day I stopped by Haggarty's to pick up a bottle of water and a paper. I always did that, and would walk home from there to cool down. I got my water and my paper and went to the register to pay for it. Right at the moment the girl started to ring me up the register died. It made this little "eeee" sound and went dark. At the same time the lights on the soda machines went dark. I thought we'd blown a fuse, but then I looked outside. The girl at the counter did, too, and we both just stood there and stared through the window at the street outside.

You know what sunlight looks like, right? Of course you do. And you know what it looks like when a cloud goes in front of the sun. This was — how can I describe it? — something in between. The whole street outside was lit with a sort of metallic-looking light. I looked at the girl, and she looked at me, and then we both went outside to see what was going on. There were already some people coming out of stores and things and all staring up at the sky.

Now, here is the part where they usually start nodding and giving me those sympathetic smiles. One dirty look out of you and this story is done. Period. Just listen.

The sky was gone. I tell you, it was just gone! Way high up there was a big expanse of white with dark shafts cutting across it. If you looked off toward the horizon you could see walls, dim with haze because of the distance, but they were definitely walls, and there was even a door, a big dark rectangle about in the same spot Mount Rainier should have been. Stretching halfway across the sky was a pair of long, thin lines of bright, glaring light. That's why the lighting in the street looked so odd. It was just starting to hit me that those were fluorescent bulbs and that they had to be as big as redwood trees, when I heard someone scream behind me, "Oh, God, look!" and I did.

At the other end of town, and I am never going to forget this until the day I die, there were two giants. They weren't just ordinary giants, either. They were animals, sort of. More like cartoons characters. One was pretty much a tiger, but white instead of orange; the other one was a weird greenish-black rabbit. You know, like Bugs Bunny, standing there on two legs and looking down at us with his arms folded, and smiling. God, the look in their eyes gave me chills. It was the same look you see on a kid who is about to soak a frog in gasoline and then light a match. They were huge – no, huge doesn't even begin to describe it. I figure that they both could've looked at each other over the roof of a twenty-story building. They were standing just outside of town, and we could only see them from the knees up. They were dressed, at least at first, in the baggy kind of clothes that teenagers wear in school, and they were just standing there.

We stared at them. They stared back at us, and then they looked at each other and grinned. The rabbit said something to the tiger. It took a good three or four seconds for the sound to reach us, but by the time it did all we heard was a low rumble that made the windows shimmy. They looked back down at us, and then they started to get undressed.

What could we do? We all just stood and watched, totally stunned, like we were seeing some kind of bizarre movie being projected on the sky, while they dropped their pants and stepped out of them, then tugged off their shirts and tossed them out of sight. They stood over us naked, all huge and lithe and furry and grinning, and then all at once they stepped forward and started destroying our town.

The rabbit went one way while the tiger came straight toward us. The weird light was glinting off of his fangs and he was staring right at me.

I watched him come straight across the buildings on D Street where the big tourist hotel is – was, sorry. His legs were just smashing right through them and kicking up a gigantic cloud of debris. I watched them come apart, roofs and walls shattering and flying up into the air, and right away in my head I was back in Oklahoma watching a big mother of a tornado ripping up Catoosa. It was exactly the same scene, except this twister was striped black and white. My old instincts to take cover kicked in and I turned and ran back into the store. There's no doubt in my mind that it saved my life. There was no basement and the back room was locked, so I just pressed my back against the wall and hoped for the best.

I could hear him coming – boom, boom, boom, with the floor shaking under me and the sound of buildings crashing making my ears ring. Outside the people that I'd been standing with were still standing there, kind of hunched over, and taking slow, tiny steps backward while they kept looking up higher and higher. They were like a whole herd of deer caught in the headlights of a truck. The crashing got louder; they kept retreating in baby steps, and then the street got darker. All at once they screamed and threw their arms up and started to fall down. Just a half-second later I saw a foot, a big furry foot, bigger than a semi truck come crashing down from above and land right on top of them. The whole store shook and things came tumbling down off of the shelves on either side of me. Strangely enough, I don't recall hearing any sound. The whole thing had for a few seconds turned into a silent movie, this giant foot sinking into the street, the pavement cracking all around it and dust flying up, and then the foot bending forward and sweeping up out of sight.

A few of the ceiling tiles suddenly fell in and smacked to the floor on either side of me and right away I could hear again. I thought that the tiger was starting to smash up the store so I bolted for the door and ran back out into the street. What I saw there jarred me so much that I stopped short and right away barfed up last night's dinner. There was a footprint there, deep, three, maybe four times as long as this room. The people who had been standing with me were totally flat, their guts all pressed out and squished around them. I could still hear that boom-boom and I turned and saw the tiger walking away from me. There was a whole line of footprints just like this one behind him, and each one filled with bodies. He was walking right down the street, stepping on people the whole way, with his stripy tail flipping around over his ass as though he was having the time of his life.

He turned a corner after a few blocks. No, actually, he made his own corner by just turning and stepping down on the Tru-Value, then kicking his foot forward and ripping the roof up in one big piece. I didn't wait to see what he did then. I just turned and ran back into the store and hid under the counter.

I don't think I was there more than five minutes. It's hard to tell. I did it out of pure, primal instinct, that reptile part of your brain that makes you want to run and hide when there is danger. I think I pissed my pants, too, but I can barely remember. In that time I was able to collect my thoughts, get past the "this can't be happening" stage, and come to the conclusion that I had to get the hell out of town. Running was not an option. I had seen up close where that could get you. No, I had to get to my truck. I had a nice sturdy SUV, one that actually had off-road experience, not one of these yuppie wagons that they're afraid to take over a speed bump. I figured that if I could just get to my wheels, I could make a dash out of town, out into the mountains, then turn off road into one of the deep dark valleys and hide out until these two monsters got bored and went back to wherever they'd come from.

The street outside was quiet. Anyone nearby who could still run or hide had already done so. The rest, well, they were either gone already or too far gone to help. There were still noises in the distance, though, like out of a horror movie: screams, crashing sounds, big loud bangs, this deep thundery rumble that I figured out were these two big boys talking to each other, and there was no way to tell where it was coming from. The sound was bouncing off of the buildings around me, and for all I know off of those hazy walls in the far distance. The echoes were disorienting, and the buildings nearby were just tall enough that I couldn't see over them to know where the danger was. I figured that the best thing to do would be to try to stick as close to the buildings as I could, and try to make as straight a line as I could for my house. You know how a mouse scurries along the baseboard when it's trying to get away? That was me.

The first turn I took turned out to be the wrong one and I almost lost whatever was left of my dinner. The rabbit was right there, just a block away. He was down on his knees, all hunched over, and thank Heaven he was facing straight away from me. He had these big, big long feet, and the bottoms of them were just covered everywhere with blood and pieces of clothing stuck to the fur. His tail was twitching back and forth. I could swear I saw something moving under it. Oh, God...oh, god damn.

That isn't the worst of it, though. I told you that he was hunched over, right? I could see right along the road between his feet. He had a big dick hanging down, hard, like he was getting off on it all. It was swaying back and forth like a pendulum, and past it I could see that he had a whole big group of people trapped in front of him. They were scrambling around and squalling, and he had his head down right over them... ...and...

...Jesus Christ, he was eating them! You wouldn't think a rabbit would eat meat, would you, but I saw it for myself. He was scooping them up to his mouth with one hand, one and two at a time, and just swallowing them whole. I recognized some of them, people I had waved to on my way to work. I could see them going down his throat...

Oh, Jesus. Get me some water, will you? Please, I need some water.

Anyway.

There was no two ways about it: I had to get past that rabbit in order to get to my truck. In my dreams I could've just hotwired a car somewhere and taken off, but firstly, I don't have the faintest idea how to hotwire a car, and secondly, most of them that I could see had either been rolled over or smashed outright by one or the other of the giants. No, the only way that I could see to escape depended on my truck. I wish I didn't have to watch what was happening in the next block, but I didn't have much choice. I had to wait until the rabbit's head was facing a little to the right so he would have the least likelihood of catching sight of me behind him, and when I saw my chance I just charged across the street and ducked behind a mailbox on the other side.

The rabbit just kept on eating, all peaceful, like he was grazing on a handful of lettuce. I kept going.

I had to run a zigzag course since there was no street that cut straight diagonally across town, so it was up one, over one, up one, over one. I didn't want to spend too much time on any one street, especially with what I had seen on Monroe Avenue. Oh, Lord. See, a few of the streets were empty, but most of them had people running through them. I ran into a couple of hundred people on Monroe, probably out of that big tourist hotel – Pine Crest? Pine Cone? Pine something. There was nobody directing them; it was every man for himself. I don't know why, but at the time it seemed like a good idea to join them. I guess it's a herd-mentality sort of thing. Safety in numbers, right? They were going my way so I turned the corner and ran with them.

God, was that ever a mistake. We didn't get half a block before the tiger jumped out in front of us. He came flying through the air from behind the bank building and landed on both feet, BOOM, and stood there grinning at us for a second while we all tried to stop. A fellow ahead of me turned around just as someone slammed into my back and smacked me up right against him. He put his arms around me and started squeezing me in a bear hug, all the while letting out this awful high-pitched scream like some sort of animal. Oddly enough, I think that by holding me up like that he kept me alive, because all around us people were getting knocked off their feet and going down in big heaps.

Then BOOM again, and the whole street shook. I looked over my shoulder, and there was the rabbit standing there behind us. He still had a giant hard-on that was bobbing in front of him as he straightened up, and he put his hand on it and started stroking himself as he looked down at us all trapped between him and the tiger. I wasn't about to wait around to see what he had in mind, but I couldn't break free. The guy holding me was still screaming and blubbering, and as much as I tried to kick free he wouldn't let go.

The crowd was going completely insane all around me. Can you blame them? I turned forward in time to see the tiger take a big step forward, bend down, and reach down into the street in front of me. His hand plowed through the people and pushed them into a big pile, then closed around them and lifted them all up into the air. I don't know how many he caught, fifteen maybe. I could see their arms and legs kicking around from between his fingers as he held them in front of his face.

His fist closed tighter. The muscles of his forearm bulged. I cannot even begin to describe the noise they made as he crushed them all like a handful of grapes, with juice squirting out all over and splattering against his muzzle.

I did not have to see any more. Remember how I said it was every man for himself? You will do the most god awful things when it comes to saving your own skin. There was no time to worry about the dumb fuck that was hanging onto me. I brought both my arms up and smashed my fists down as hard as I could on his collarbone, snapping it on both sides. His arms went limp and I pushed him away as soon as my feet hit the ground. Ahead, the tiger opened his hand and turned it toward us, like he was saying, "Look what I'm going to do to you," but I was too busy looking around for someplace to run to. There was no way out forward or back without running into one of the boys. All the doors on either side of us were closed and locked, although that did not stop a few desperate people from standing there and beating on them. The only hope I could see was a little cellar window that stood open at the bottom of one of the buildings to my right. It couldn't have been more than eighteen inches wide, but at the time it was the only likely way out.

There were people all around me that I just shoved aside while I headed for that opening, and as for the people on the ground, I just ran right over them. Thank God I never developed a gut like my father had or I would have never fit into that little window. I dove headfirst through it, hit the floor of the cellar and rolled to my feet. Behind me there were a couple of people who looked like they wanted to follow my lead, clawing their way toward the window behind me. I stepped back farther to make room for them, but just as they got to the sidewalk I saw what looked like a white wall with black stripes dropping down from above. I tried to shout at them to move faster, but it wouldn't have done any good, even if I could've gotten the words out in time. The tiger's hand came down sideways right in front of the window. When it lifted again there was nobody behind it.

For a minute or two I thought about hiding out where I was. It was that same instinct to duck and cover, but this time I fought it off. The tiger had grabbed those people right as they were about to dive through the window, which meant that he knew there was an escape route there, and for all I knew he had seen me go through first. That meant that at any second he and his friend would probably start tearing the building apart to try to dig me out. Not me, Brother! In less than two seconds I was up the stairs and out the back door, which opened up into a long, thin alley. I could still hear the most sickening sounds coming from the next street, but at least that meant that the boys were still preoccupied. I think I'm going to go to Hell for saying that I was overjoyed to keep hearing those sounds behind me as I made my getaway, and was madly disappointed when I could not hear them any longer.

Now I was facing a dilemma. Clearly I couldn't just sprint for home; any time I ran into other people I would be in danger of getting swept up in a noisy mob that would attract the giants' attention. On the other hand, I couldn't afford to waste time, because at their size it would not take those boys long to level the entire town, and me with it. I found myself in the bizarre position of having to avoid both the giants *and* the people of Opal. I decided it was safer to stick to the back alleys and driveways as much as I could rather than risk being out in the open. That slowed me down quite a bit but after what I had seen, I think I would rather have had a house get pushed over onto me than let myself be spotted. Before long I settled into a routine of rushing through the middle of the block, then stopping just shy of the main road and peeking around both corners to make sure the coast was clear of both big furry boys and frightened, fleeing Opalites.

That technique was the third thing that saved my life that day, because when I got to the corner of Richland, two blocks from my house, I came upon the tiger. He was facing my way, and I'm sure that if I had just run around the corner he would have noticed me for sure. As it was, he was too busy having his sick fun with some more of my poor neighbors. Saint Xavier's – Saint X, we called it – used to stand on the corner, a big old stone church. There was nothing left of it. The stones were all crumbled in a big pile that had been shoved across Richland Avenue. The tiger was standing in front of it, stretching up into the sky like a redwood tree. At his feet there were more people. I don't think I knew any of them but it was hard to tell at that point. He was urinating on them. He had his pecker in his hand and was standing there smirking while he hosed them down, aiming on purpose at anyone who was trying to get up and knocking them around like bowling pins. Some of them were still moving; a lot had stopped for good.

When he was done pissing he shook off and then turned around. The whole back side of him, backs of his legs, his ass and even his balls were all bright red, like he'd sat in wet paint. I watched around the corner with just one eye, trying to stay hidden, as he stepped over the pile of rubble that had been Saint X and used his toes to rake it back behind him. Tons of boulders and steel and wood went rolling back over the people and buried them all, and when he was done the tiger just stepped out of my sight, and I could hear more crashing and more screaming.

Luckily he had moved away from my house. I only had two blocks to go, but I made a big detour around the back of Henry Avenue and went that way instead. The smell of cat pee was stifling, and besides, I couldn't bring myself to go past that scene.

Both my house and my truck were intact, but I couldn't say the same for the houses across the street. They were totally flat, their roofs sitting all shattered atop the wreckage. You could tell that they'd been crushed straight down from above. If I still had any thoughts of trying to hide out in my basement they went out the window right there. I ran inside, grabbed the keys off the hook, jumped into the truck, and headed out onto Richland.

Now, if this were a movie, I'd get out onto the highway, look back in my rearview mirror and see both boys still merrily romping through the town, and then floor it and head for safety while the credits rolled. No such luck. See, the problem with my plan was that I wasn't the only one to come up with it. As I got to the spot where Richland opened up to Route Four Ninety I ran right into a big traffic jam. The idiots were squeezing single-file between an overturned station wagon on the left and the hurricane fence that ran along the right side of the road. I leaned out the window and looked around, but couldn't see any giant furry monsters in sight. Maybe if there had been these people would have been spurred into action, but for some reason – shock, maybe, or just plain ignorance – they were lining up like lemmings all trying to merge into that one lane.

If you're going to buy an SUV, buy a Ford. They can go through anything. Mine went through the hurricane fence in four wheel drive and kept right on going. I left a hubcap behind and probably both of my headlights, but who cares? I spun out onto the highway and joined the trickle of refugees who had made it past the blockade. In my rearview mirror I could see the rest of my cars following my lead. I started to feel like Moses. You know, "Follow me, Children of

Israel," that sort of thing. I let out a whoop and started beating on the steering wheel and laughing like an idiot. Even so, I wasn't about to forget what I was running from, and I kept glancing in the rearview mirror, scared that at any minute I'd see a big shadow on the horizon chasing after me.

Here is the ironic part. You're going to laugh. See, I had a rabbit's foot hanging from my rearview mirror. I figured it would bring me good luck. I was staring into the mirror, with the rabbit's foot swaying just under my line of sight, when around the mirror I suddenly saw a big dark shape appear. It didn't just appear; it dropped out of the sky like a battleship falling across the highway. I hit the brakes hard and started to fishtail, and finally wound up spinning clear around three-sixty. Ahead of me I watched brake lights come on and tires smoke before the cars smashed up against the side of a rabbit's foot a million times bigger than the one on my mirror. I had seen that same foot before with little people squashed like bugs against its sole. Now there it was, standing like a big furry wall across the whole width of the highway, with no way around it for the steep embankments at its toes and at its heel. I could see the black silhouette of his leg rising up into the sky and disappearing at the top of my windshield right around the level of his knee.

Two cars spun out on either side of me. Once again my old tornado safety training kicked in. If you're in a vehicle and one of those mothers is coming for you, you get out and you get down. That was the fourth thing that saved my life, only looking back on it now I'm sorry that it did. I think I would have been a lot happier if I had ended up like the rest of Opal.

I wasn't thinking about that at the time, of course. The only thing going through my reptilian brain was to save my skin. I jumped out of the truck, dodged a big station wagon that was swerving out of control alongside of me, and made a dash for the embankment. The idea in a tornado, of course, is to get down low, and that was the one thought that was going through my mind. I was familiar with that area from the hikes I used to take. On the other side of the embankment on my left was the lake – no cover there. On the right, though, the embankment rose up and then fell into a deep, deep ravine. I figured that if I could get my ass down there, those big bastards would never find me. I'd be a needle in a haystack to them.

You know how they talk about the best laid plans of mice and men? Well, I was the mouse. A very small, very powerless mouse that was only just then starting to realize what he was up against. The embankment was soggy from the rains we had all the week before. I was scrambling and sliding the whole way, my fingers tearing up big clods of grass and leaving skid marks in the mud, but finally I got to the top. I was expecting to see that nice deep ravine dropping below me, and I could just slide right down the hill and curl up at the bottom among the trees and be safe at last.

Instead, I found myself standing on the edge of a cliff and looking out into infinity.

You don't know what I mean? Here, imagine this. You're standing in a big aircraft hangar at night, with all of its fluorescent lights on, and you're staring at a wall that looks like it's a mile way. That's kind of how it felt. When I looked down I could see a floor way below me with carpeting stretching for miles, and when I leaned over to look down further my head hit a wall. That is, it felt like a wall. Maybe it was made of glass or something, but I couldn't see it, not a bit of it. There was no reflection like glass would make, and when I smacked it with my fist it didn't make any noise at all. The top of the embankment just...stopped, and there was the wall keeping me from jumping and taking my chances. I stood up on my toes, even hopped up a few times to see if I could feel a top edge, but there was nothing.

Nothing. Nothing to do but turn around and watch the slaughter.

The rabbit was standing with his arms folded, all smug. The highway below was turning into a demolition derby with cars spinning out and crashing into each other. Here and there people would try to get out, only to be mowed down by other cars rushing past them. They were spinning around in circles, riding up onto the embankments, then spinning around again and trying to go back the other way.

Why? Because the tiger was there, too. He was standing about a half mile back or so, in the same posture the rabbit was in. Both of them were staring down at the cars wheeling and skidding and smashing into one another, and both of them were laughing and talking to each other in their thunder-rumble voices. I think I can imagine what they were saying. "Look at that, we don't even have to do anything to make them die!"

Then the rabbit bent down all of a sudden and picked up one of those little Toyota cars, the round kind, that was spinning its wheels in the mud on the shoulder. I saw faces behind the windows and hands smacking against the glass. The rabbit eyed the car for just a second, turned it over a few times in his hand, and then turned toward the lake and hurled the car sidearm straight over the embankment. From my spot on the high ground I could see the car skip across the surface of the water, tumbling over five or six times before it finally splashed to a stop and sank under the surface. The tiger let out a roar that hurt my ears and pumped his arm, then bent down and snatched up a car of his own. He threw it the same way into the water; it only bounced once before all four doors flew open, the passengers went sailing out, and they and the car all disappeared into the lake. The rabbit-boy laughed and grabbed another car.

They took turns like this, I guess five or six throws each, and then got bored and turned their attention to the traffic jam boiling between them. The rabbit held out his arm and made a gesture – well, I can't show you with my wrists tied, but it was like an umpire saying, "You're out!" Just like that, a wave of his hand, and every one of the cars disappeared. Pop! Just like that, gone in a wink. Where the stalled cars had been there were people still sitting, drivers dazed with their hands up like they were still holding the wheel. Where cars had still been moving people were now flying, landing on the pavement and rolling to a stop. That's when the boys decided to snuff them out, just for the fun of it. They started to walk toward each other, the boys did, and they were being very deliberate about crushing the people like a bunch of bugs under their feet. The ones who could still walk were scrambling for the embankments, but they were so muddied up and slick by then that there was no hope of climbing up to where I was. I sat and watched while the people were squashed to death, these massive feet chasing them around as they ran for their lives and then coming down and grinding them into the ground. It was all so methodical, and so twisted, the boys grinning and wagging their tails and stroking their cocks while blood squirted up between their toes.

There must have been a couple hundred to start with. Then there were a hundred. Then fifty, then thirty. The whole stretch of highway was covered with little broken bodies surrounded by bright-red starbursts. At one point I heard the pap-pap of gunshots and saw one little buckaroo trying to fight back, God bless him, with flashes coming from what I guess was a pistol in his hand. The tiger saw him, laughed, bent down and picked him up, and then while the man screamed the tiger pulled him apart, one limb at a time, tossing first each piece, and then what was left over his shoulder. There was no more fighting back after that, and the last of the survivors were herded together and crushed all at once beneath the rabbit's heel.

That was when I suddenly realized, what the hell are you doing? You're standing here and gawking while there's open road ahead. Who knows how far you could go before you hit that wall? If you're lucky you can get behind them and they'll turn and head back into Opal without ever noticing you! Jesus, was I an idiot. I'd wasted all that precious time staring at what was happening, just like a train wreck where you can't look away. God damn it!

So I started to run along the top of the embankment, which in hindsight was probably the stupidest damned thing I'd ever done in my life, next to not having gotten my ass out of there when the two were distracted. The tiger's face turned toward me. I saw his eyes focus and he pointed my way. Son of a bitch! There wasn't anything else I could do except keep running, all the while throwing glances back to see if they were following me.

At first they just stood there, watching me skitter like a roach along the crest of the hill. I thought at first that they were actually going to let me go. No such luck. They let me run about a quarter mile, I guess, and then I saw the rabbit bend his legs and crouch way down, and then suddenly he leaped straight up into the air, a hundred feet or more. He looked like a rocket taking off, until he reached the top of his jump and came back down hard. Both of his feet hit the ground at the same time and a shock wave started to rush out away from the crater he made. I let out a yell and poured on as much speed as I could, but in a few seconds I heard the roar of the impact, and a split-second later the ground lurched under my feet and sent me flipping into the air. I landed on the slope and started to roll down, utterly unable to stop myself. The water in the soil had been jarred to the surface, and by the time I rolled to the bottom I was caked with mud six inches thick.

When I finally stopped I was as dizzy as all get-out, so when I first tried to stand up I fell right over again. Then I heard it, a sound I'd heard before, and it sent a jolt of panic through me. Boom-boom-boom. The ground quivered under me, and when I sat up I saw four giant size-feet, two long rabbit ones and two striped tiger ones, crashing toward me. They were walking side by side, both leering down at me with killing in their eyes.

I struggled to my feet but found that I could hardly move. My jogging suit had turned into a mud suit that was weighing me down like lead. The two giants were getting closer. With no time to spare I tore off my sweat shirt, then shoved my pants down and jumped out of them. I stumbled away from them, much lighter now, buck naked. Both of them stopped for a moment as if that surprised them, and then the air itself shook with their laughter and they started toward me again. I didn't know what else to do, so I just ran, while they got bigger and bigger, and then they were right on top of me.

You know, mortal terror is a fantastic motivator. I found out that I had athletic abilities that would have won me a gold medal in dodge-ball at the Olympics. The rabbit lifted his foot over me; he was going to step on me, too, just like he had all those others. I stopped and stood still as it came down, and then just as it blocked out the sight of his face I charged to the side and ran for all I was worth. I broke out into the unnatural light just an instant before I heard a powerful crash behind me, and another wave ran through the ground and made me stagger.

I spun around and looked up just in time to see his expression go from smug to startled. I crouched and waited while he lifted his foot again and once again it glided over me, filling the whole sky. I took a chance and started to rush straight back toward his toes, then cut to the left. I was gambling that he would guess wrongly, and he did. His foot moved to the right at the last moment and slammed down next to me. The shock sent me flying off of my feet, and I landed hard on the pavement.

There wasn't much more than a second for me to recover before I saw the tiger's foot coming down toward me. His was wider, the toes covering more distance than I could probably run with the speed that they were falling. My mind was working overtime, and without any time to think I rushed toward his arch. It was a hell of a risk, and it paid off. There was just enough clearance over my head that I didn't get much more than a bump before I rolled out next to his foot. I wound up on my back and saw them both looming over me. Both of them were hard, and were grinning down at me past these big, fat erections. I still cannot believe that these monsters could be getting such enjoyment at my expense, not to mention the expense of Opal.

The tiger's foot started to move. I thought, "Oh, shit!" and rolled to my feet. My body was all bruised and I was starting to get winded. Looking up while running was making me dizzy and I was stumbling more and more. The rabbit's foot suddenly appeared out of nowhere and smashed down right in front of me, so close that I ran right into it and bounced off like a rubber ball. I spun and started to race the other way. The tiger's foot came down hard on my left, and when I angled away its mate came crashing down on my right, sending me stumbling back in the other direction. That was when I realized that the rules of the game had changed. They were not trying to kill me any longer. They were toying with me, chasing me around and making me run for their amusement.

No way, I thought. No absolutely fucking way. I'd had enough. I stopped dead in my tracks and stood perfectly still. The rabbit's foot landed, ka-boom, in front of me. I had to fight to keep my balance, but when I was steady again I turned and looked up at him, looked him dead on, and shot him the finger. "Come on, you big asshole!" I shouted, "Playtime's over!" It was a perfect John Wayne Moment, and as it turns out, it was the second stupidest thing I've ever done in my life.

The tiger raised his foot. Its underside was covered with man-stains and I figured that I was about to become one of them. The rabbit, though, put his hand on his friend's chest and the tiger stopped, and then put his foot back down slowly with a look of disappointment. The rabbit looked down at me, just stared for a long moment, while I stood there with my middle finger poking up at him, and then he started to bend down. His hand swept down toward me – God, was it ever huge. I dropped my arm down and took a few steps back out of sheer instinct, but damned if I was going to give him the satisfaction of making me run again. His fingers came down, thumb and forefinger on both sides of me, and then pinched together. It was like a furry vice! He had my arms pinned tight against my sides and was squeezing my ribcage so hard I was sure it was going to pop. My guts fell down through my feet as he hauled me up into the air. I never did like heights, and the ground was dropping away fast.

The next thing I knew I was staring right into his eye. It was bigger than my whole head, way bigger, and the most bizarre color of purple you'd ever seen.

Yeah, I know, green rabbit with purple eyes. Don't look at me like that – remember our deal.

It was bigger than my whole head, and purple around the iris. The pupil itself was almost like a black mirror. I could see my face reflected in it. It didn't move at all, didn't even twitch. He just studied me, right up close. Of all the horrible things I saw that day, as strange as this might sound, I am sure that sight is the one that haunts my nightmares the worst.

After a while he said something. I don't know what it was, since like I said, both of their voices were just rumbles, but after he said it he lowered me down to his mouth. I knew for sure that he was going to eat me and I started to kick and shout, "No, please!" and other foolheaded things like that. His lips opened – he had fangs, I tell you, not just rabbit teeth but fangs as well – and then this big pink tongue rolled out and dragged up the front of my body. God damn, have you ever been licked by a rabbit? Do you know how utterly soft and smooth their tongues are? Now imagine that sliding over your *whole fucking body!* He licked me again, and then a third time. My head was spinning. I couldn't believe that I was starting to get turned on by it. How can someone get a boner when he's facing death like that? They say that a lot of times, men who are hanged will shoot a load of cum just as they die. Maybe this was something like that. But whatever the reason, I was getting hard, even though I was scared completely out of my wits.

He licked me one more time, number four, and then lifted me away from his face a little, gave me this bizarrely sweet smile, and tilted me downward. I saw the top of the tiger's head below me. He was on his knees. The rabbit's dick was in his mouth. I could only stare as he worked on it, moving it in and out, and then he pulled back, let the big thing flop free, and looked up at me. His mouth opened, and the rabbit started to lower me toward it. I could see all the way down into his throat, big teeth framing a black pit. I panicked then – who wouldn't? – and started to kick and thrash with every bit of strength I had, but it was no use. I was lowered closer and closer while the tiger waited patiently, his tail flicking and swaying behind him. I guess I was about thirty feet or so away when the rabbit suddenly let go of me. I fell, screaming the whole way, straight down into the tiger's mouth and into his throat, and everything got dark.

I landed on something soft and started to thrash and scream, thinking I was in his stomach. But no – there was light above me. I stopped screaming and sat up, looked all around, and realized that I had landed in a garbage dumpster. There were brick walls rising up on both sides, and sunlight – natural sunlight, not the fluorescent glow I'd been seeing all day – streaming down between them.

I think you know the rest of the story. Running out into the street, naked, covered with stinking garbage, screaming and crying. Cops waving batons and barking into their radios. Pepper spray. Tasers. Handcuffs and shackles, and finally this cozy bed with the leather cuffs and the video camera watching me. Hi, Guys. How're you doing in there?

So that's my side of the story. I guess I can see how you'd prefer your version. You see, in your version, the citizens of Opal were just victims of mindless, unfeeling forces of nature. It's comforting, I know, to imagine that there is no malevolence behind any of it. It is good to believe that nobody is judging you, and to believe that you are something a little more than just a playtoy for a force so savage and cruel that it giggles and masturbates while it tortures you to death.

What does it matter in the end, though? My version or your version, you are just as dead. The only difference is that in my version, you might be one of the unlucky ones who are just amusing enough that you are worth saving for another day, another game. I know that's why I'm here. They haven't gotten all the fun out of me that they are going to, and they are simply waiting until they get bored again and want something fun to play with.

If I were you, I wouldn't want to be around when they decide to come and get me.

Can't Spell Slaughter Without Laughter

Mostly for us it was darkness, heavy with the stink of fear. We were all deathly silent, listening, as though we had a choice, to the horrible screams that echoed from the world outside of our prison. Sometimes they went on for long, long minutes; others for only a few seconds, but all of them ended abruptly and always right at their peak. That was our signal to move to the center, to tense our bodies, hold our breaths, and wait for the lid of our prison to be lifted to reveal that long, grinning muzzle high above. Thick furry fingers would thrust themselves among us while we writhed and thrashed, fighting to save ourselves from their clutches. It was each for himself then. There was no cooperation as the massive digits groped about among us, eventually capturing one or two or three and hoisting them, howling, up and out of sight. Then the lid would close, and the awful screams would start anew.

I only caught a brief glimpse of the monster before he caught me. He was right on the brink of stallionhood, with a massive chest and shoulders that still bore the leanness of youth. Big, too, and how I did not hear him coming is a mystery. I did not get more than three steps away before his hand closed around me and I was dumped into a box with what must have been more than a hundred others.

Less than half of that were left.

The lid opened again without any warning. Our captor's face appeared, big square teeth grinning cruelly, a screaming woman clamped helplessly between them. His hand dropped down into our midst, herded two more of us into a corner and scooped them up, and the lid snapped shut. The screaming continued, punctuated by a deep and bone-shaking thunder. Not many who were still alive knew that sound, but I had heard it before from others of his kind. It was laughter, rolling up from the depths of a chest as vast as a rail station. It did not stop when the screams did; in fact, it only grew louder.

Inevitably it came to my turn. I fought hard, shoving at the others who were shoving back at me with equal desperation. The groping fingers slapped against me and sent me stumbling into the wall of the box, then slammed me hard into the corner. I tried to squirm past them but they clamped tightly around my left leg and hoisted me up. My body flopped upside down as the upturned faces of the other captives dropped away, and I was bathed in brilliant, dazzling light.

In a few seconds my eyes adjusted enough to allow me to take in the full horror of the killing field below. The room was vast and empty. Something like newspaper covered the floor from corner to corner. Huge, bloody hoofprints were everywhere, and everywhere too was what was left of the dozens of other captives. Most were unrecognizable, nothing more than flattened skin and smears of red; here, though, I could see a body torn in two, its face frozen in its final agonies; there, limbs plucked from a torso and tossed glibly aside; over there, a pile of guts still steaming. Midway up the wall a female gaped through dead eyes, her twisted corpse embedded deep within a splatter of thick gray ooze.

The world spun wildly as I was flipped suddenly upright. Two rough fingers pinched around my midsection, squeezing hard as they held me before the colt's face. His eyes were huge and dark. Perhaps they would have seemed sweet and soulful to one his size. To me, though, they burned with an indescribable disdain, reflected a lustful dominance that struck me almost like a physical force. He smiled — no, not a smile, but a grimace, and when he did I saw that his teeth were red, and when they parted I could briefly see shreds of mashed flesh pressed into their crushing surfaces before he clashed them together again. Then he hauled me to his eye and gazed closely at my face.

I knew what he wanted. I had seen it before. He wanted me to scream, to beg for my life. While I was dangling upside-down I had caught sight of his gargantuan penis standing stiff and erect. I was meant to be his entertainment, my cries of pain his reward. I resolved that, no matter how horrific my fate, I would not give him that satisfaction, and thus I remained silent.

I had hoped that he would be disappointed and simply dispatch me quickly, but instead the air was shaken with that familiar rumble — laughter, savage and cruel, pounding in my ears like a thousand drums. His black eyes narrowed and his grin grew ferocious, and then all at once I was dropping through the air. My gorge rose as the corpse-strewn floor rushed up toward me.

My descent halted so abruptly that it nearly snapped my neck — and, oh, how I wish it had. The huge fingers that had caught me now carried me down and spilled me onto the floor, and the colt stood up tall over me. Reaching out with one hand he braced himself upon the wall, and slowly he raised a mighty hoof over me while eying me with the contempt with which one might eye a disgusting insect. So this would be it. He would crush me right then and there, and with me dead he would simply select another plaything. The bottom of his hoof was caked with raw meat, as I was far from the first to have died this way. I readied myself for the end.

The hoof came down slowly, steadily. I stood my ground, watching it grow larger and larger. I wanted to scream but stubbornly remained silent. I wanted to run, to cower, but I forced myself to stand fast and wait for the pain which I hoped would be brief. I could no longer see his expression, just the great round hoof with the face of a former victim still recognizable among the mess packed into its center.

Then it came down fast and hard, not upon but beside me, the impact loud enough to pop my left eardrum and send me flying off of my feet. The crash echoed and was followed by another storm of heartless laughter. The game was not over then, no, far from it. Shaking, I raised my eyes in time to see the colt towering over me, his mammoth erection jutting straight forth like the boom of a crane. Horses are built impressively enough when eye to eye with one and this one was no exception, but at a hundred feet tall the sight is positively daunting – particularly when its owner abruptly squats down over you.

The sight of that immense slab rushing toward me overwhelmed my senses. Raw survival instinct took over and I made a frantic leap to the side. Behind me tons of flesh slapped down to the ground with a noise like a cannon shot. A meaty ripple ran through the whole length from the impact, and from its flared tip came a brief gush of thin, clear syrup. Another rumble of laughter assaulted my ears as I struggled to my feet. Sneering down at me, the giant gripped his member about its base and hefted it like a club.

Reeling, I leaped away again, and then again, and yet again as the great penis slammed down repeatedly, landing first in front of me, then behind, each time missing me only by inches. I felt like a grasshopper frantically dodging this way and that while the barbarous young giant sought to smash me beneath his malehood. Throughout it all his laughter tore through the air, louder even than the crashing of his great organ.

There is no telling how much longer the grim game would have gone on had I not on one very narrow escape landed squarely in the pool of fluid that had squirted forth on the first impact. My feet hit with a thick splash and instantly swept out from beneath me, slamming me down flat on my back in the center of the puddle. Without thinking I rolled over and tried to get up, and soon found myself covered head to toe. It had the weight and slickness of motor oil and every effort to regain my feet only left me skittering and flailing.

My giant captor was shaking with mirth, reddened teeth glistening and chomping as he guffawed at how helpless I was. I had to clamp my hands over my ears to keep from being deafened until at last the thunder subsided to a wicked and ominous chuckle. A big hoof thudded down on my left nearby, and then the other on the right. I managed somehow to gain control once more over my terror and fought down the urge to flee, knowing that my flailing about in the slippery fluid would only amuse the titan further.

Rolling to my back I saw him standing over me as before, his head canted to the side so that he could observe me past the colossal erection that swayed and bobbed so ponderously overhead. Again he crouched for what I thought would be the killing blow, but that game, it seemed, had grown tiresome. I watched as his leg muscles bunched and bulged, his body sinking lower until all I could see was the enormous bulk of his testicles looming overhead. Each was the size of a small car and falling fast. I bit back a scream of terror and instead threw my arms up as the colt's scrotum landed upon me like a circus tent falling, the big globes rolling languidly to either side.

The weight was unbearable, the musky stench overwhelming. I gasped like a fish out of water, barely able to gulp in enough air to stay conscious. The colt knew it, too, and made a new game of it, leaning forward so that his heavy scrotum rolled suffocatingly over my face. At that my body reacted instinctively and I began to writhe and wiggle and fight for air, which from the sound of his groans must have thrilled him tremendously. When my struggles began to weaken he simply leaned back again, granting me just enough breath to keep me alive before he smothered me once more.

I nearly passed out five or six times before the game evolved again. The huge sac lifted slightly off of me and dragged forward, and when it came down again I felt an unbearable weight upon my legs. I realized that he had sat on them, and that they were spared from being crushed outright only for having fallen within the cleft between his buttocks. I could hardly be grateful for that small mercy since now the full weight of his scrotum was upon me, squashing me brutally down against the floor. I felt my ribcage bending, beginning to give way. Another second and I would have been just another mutilated corpse amidst the multitude.

The crushing weight, however, rose up and away with a sudden rush of cool air. Stunned and gasping I sat up, only to feel my legs jerked upward, sending my head and shoulders cracking painfully back on the floor. I saw the colt's hooves rise up and hover in the air high overhead as he settled flat on his back. The vast bulk of his rump now stretched before me, my feet clenched tightly between the powerful cheeks. He meant to hold me but I could feel my legs sliding, still slick with his spilled fluids, and with a defiant shout I started to kick and squirm to free myself.

A trio of thick, blunt fingers appeared and clamped around my slippery torso, fumbling for a firm grip. The great slabs of muscle before me relaxed and parted; the colt's legs rose higher, and I was horrified to see the great black ring of his anus twitching eagerly as my legs were lifted toward it.

Any thoughts of noble defiance evaporated. "No!" I howled. "Please, not that!"

His fingers shifted to catch my flailing legs and pinched them tightly together. Unable to kick, my feet were pressed firmly against the center of that terrible orifice. It was warm and quivered as my slickened feet rubbed against it, and then I felt ominous pressure surrounding them. I gawked at the sight of my legs being engulfed by the black flesh. "Please! Stop it! Let me go!"

The only reply was a low grunt and a long sigh. The colt's anus clenched suddenly and painfully around my calves and then relaxed, and its rim slid smoothly up along my thighs to my waist as his fingers crammed me relentlessly inside. "Help!" I shrieked. "Someone help me! Help me!"

My voice was all but lost in the din of the colt's contented groaning. The words echoed feebly through the vast room, heard only by those damned souls still cowering in the box and awaiting their own horrific executions.

The black ring stretched around my hips and then squeezed again, sucking my slippery body in to the waist. My breath rushed out in a hoarse wheeze as my torso was compressed. "Kill yourselves!" I croaked as loud as I could manage. "For God's sake, don't let him catch you alive!"

All at once the colt's fingers released my torso and I thrust my hands down against the ring in a frantic attempt to push myself free. I did not realize that it was a trap, for the very moment my arms stopped flailing about his rough fingers pinched them to my sides and pushed me further in. I wailed as I felt the fleshy warmth sliding up over my arms, over my belly and then my chest. The fingers released me a second time and rose out of sight, and the horrible orifice grew taut while smooth flesh within it gripped and pulled, sucking me in to my shoulders. Appalled, I kicked and twisted with all my might, slipping out almost to my waist before I was hauled in again by another squeeze, this time nearly to my chin.

There was the sound of the box being opened and then of shrill screams, and above me the gigantic scrotum began to shift ponderously up and down; apparently I was not to be the only participant in this degenerate game. I could waste no time pondering the fate of others, however, fixated as I was on my own predicament. I fought wildly, howling like a madman each time I was pulled inside and wiggling with all my strength to work my way back out, too stricken by panic to catch on that I was giving him exactly what he wanted.

My mind reeled, a thousand voices babbling in my head at once. The giant had made me into a toy, a plaything for his most grotesque pleasures. The depths of such depravity were beyond comprehension. Killing us was one thing – the Beasts did that every day, as we were merely pests to them after all – but to torment us in this fashion went beyond all reason, beyond simple hatred for our kind. Clearly there were monsters even among the giants.

The colt's rectal muscles dragged me in again and my chin hit the rim of his anus, snapping my head back, and there I was held firm and fast. Before me, upside-down, I suddenly saw two enormous white paws. One toe rested on the severed head of a past victim, then cocked and idly flicked it away. The paws led up to towering legs, male by the look of the musculature. The colt's massive testicles blocked my view of the rest of the newcomer, but I had seen all that I needed to. The only sound in the room was the tiny, far-off shrieks of my fellow toys. Gone was the colt's panting and groaning; gone was his hellish laughter.

Now it was my turn to laugh, hard and lunatic. "Busted!" I shouted. "Caught red-handed, you sick bastard!" I kicked him inside. "Let's see you explain your way out of this one!"

Explain he did, or so I imagined. Their voices were too deep, the timbre far too low for our ears to make sense of their speech, but I knew from the vibrations in the flesh around me that the colt was speaking. He was answered by another thundering voice. My fellow playthings were still screaming. "Quiet, you lot!" I yelled. "I want to hear what this fucker has to say for himself."

The white paws stepped backward and then two great knees landed with a jarring boom. A vast expanse of white fur caught the light and briefly dazzled me, and when my vision cleared I found it filled by the sight of a broad dome of flesh hovering before my face. It was tipped by a long and narrow slit from which thin fluid trickled like a mountain spring.

"Oh, no..."

It mashed hard against my head, my face stuffed rudely into the depths of the spring. I felt my ears slipping into the horse's anal ring, my body sliding deeper along moist and clenching walls. In the darkness within I was deafened by the roar of the giant's blood all around, along with renewed grunts and moans of pleasure – and laughter, thunderous, hideous laughter coming now from two directions. I was shoved deep, my face pounded over and over and over by a meaty hammer. There could be no defiance now. All I could do was pray for the sweet release of death or insanity.

About the Author

Rogue is, arguably, the original macrofur. A manlike wolf who stands ninety feet tall, he came rampaging onto the scene in 1992. Stories spread around the internet about his savage assaults on cities and the fruitless attempts by humanity to drive him away, but rather than inspiring fear and panic, he created instead a cult following. Over time the stories began to evolve into tales told by Rogue himself of other giant creatures and their many misadventures. Lacking education, the ability to write and, some have argued, the capacity for coherent thought, Rogue is said to employ one or more human stenographers to transcribe his stories for him, usually in return for being removed from the menu. He is believed to reside in a cave located in the Northeastern United States, although its precise location has never been determined.

www.ingramcontent.com/pod-product-compliance
Lightning Source LLC
Chambersburg PA
CBHW051134260626
47170CB00005B/1807

* 9 7 8 1 9 3 5 5 0 9 7 9 0 *